"Am I getting too close?"
Angelia asked.

Nick's gut tightened in an annoyingly familiar reaction to her touch. "You don't know what you're getting yourself into. That's the problem. You don't think. You just jump in and hope for the best."

"That's not true. Maybe I'm a little more spontaneous than you are, but I do consider the consequences of my actions."

"Really?" His hand captured her roving fingers, stilling them against his chest so that she could feel the pounding beat of his heart through his white silk shirt. "Then you know what you're doing right now?" he asked with deadly quiet.

She let out a small gasp of air as he pulled her body against his and tilted her face upward until their lips were only inches apart. "I think so," she murmured, her heart racing with anticipation. "What about you?"

"I think . . ." He traced the outline of her jaw with his finger, his blue eyes darkening with desire. "I think I'm going crazy."

Dear Reader,

It's March—and spring is just around the corner. We all know spring is the season of love, but at Silhouette Romance, every season is romantic, and every month we offer six heartwarming stories that capture the laughter, the tears, the sheer joy of falling in love. This month is no exception!

Honey, I'm Home by Rena McKay is a delightful reminder that even the most dashing hero is a little boy at heart, and Lindsay Longford's *Pete's Dragon* will reaffirm your belief in the healing power of love...and make-believe. The intense passion of Suzanne Carey's *Navajo Wedding* will keep you spellbound, the sizzling *Two To Tango* by Kristina Logan will quite simply make you want to dance, and Linda Varner's *As Sweet as Candy* will utterly charm you.

No month is complete without our special WRITTEN IN THE STARS selection. This month we have the exciting, challenging Pisces man in Anne Peters's *Storky Jones Is Back in Town*.

Throughout the year we'll be publishing stories of love by all your favorite Silhouette Romance authors—Diana Palmer, Suzanne Carey, Annette Broadrick, Brittany Young and many, many more. The Silhouette Romance authors and editors love to hear from readers, and we'd love to hear from *you*!

Happy Reading!

Valerie Susan Hayward
Senior Editor

KRISTINA LOGAN

Two To Tango

Silhouette **Romance**

Published by Silhouette Books New York

America's Publisher of Contemporary Romance

To my mother, Pat,
for her constant encouragement and great ideas.

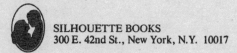

SILHOUETTE BOOKS
300 E. 42nd St., New York, N.Y. 10017

TWO TO TANGO

Copyright © 1992 by Barbara Beharry Freethy

ISBN: 0-373-08852-3

First Silhouette Books printing March 1992

All the characters in this book have no existence outside the
imagination of the author and have no relation whatsoever to
anyone bearing the same name or names. They are not even
distantly inspired by any individual known or unknown to the
author, and all incidents are pure invention.

®: Trademark used under license and registered in the United
States Patent and Trademark Office and in other countries.

Printed in the U.S.A.

Books by Kristina Logan

Silhouette Romance

Promise of Marriage #738
Hometown Hero #817
Two To Tango #852

KRISTINA LOGAN

is a native Californian and a former public-relations professional who spent several exciting years working with a variety of companies whose business interests ranged from wedding consulting to professional tennis, high technology and the film industry. Now the mother of two small children, she divides her time between her family and her first love—writing.

THE TANGO

The tango originated in the lower-class neighborhoods of Buenos Aires. The girls wore very full skirts and the men wore gaucho costumes with high-top boots and spurs. In the 1900s the dance made its way to London, Paris and eventually the United States. The original rhythm of the tango has changed from the Habanera throbbing beat to a more subdued Milonga, and the steps have become easier to do in a ballroom setting, but the dance has lost none of its flavor and creativity.

BASIC STEP

1. Slow step with left foot to left.
2. Cross right foot in front of left (slow).
3. Quick step forward with left foot.
4. Quick step to right with right foot.
5. Draw left up to right, no weight on it.

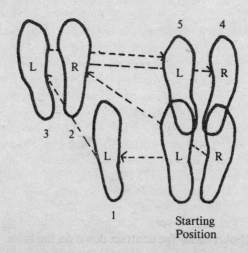

Starting
Position

Chapter One

"He's out of his mind." Nicholas Hunter stared at the contract in his hand. "What kind of a loophole is this?"

Martin Hennessey kicked his feet up on the conference table and smiled in spite of his friend's annoyance. "I'd say it's a very intriguing one."

"What the hell does that mean?"

"He's got you, Nicholas. Face facts. Juan Carlos is not going to sell you his prime Argentine coastline unless he gets what he wants."

"What he wants?" Nicholas echoed, his blue eyes widening with bewilderment. "The man wants me to dance the tango, or am I misreading this?"

Martin chuckled. "I think you've got it right."

"He's crazy. I won't do it."

"Lighten up. It's only a dance."

"This is a business deal, not some kind of a joke." Nicholas threw the contract down on the table. "I'm offering him an excellent price for his property. It's the best deal he's going to get."

"I agree."

"When I left Buenos Aires on Friday, a mere forty-eight hours ago, everything was set. You two were just going to sit down and work out the final details. Now everything has gone haywire. What happened?"

"Juan Carlos didn't like the way you acted when you were down there," Martin replied calmly. "You didn't socialize with anyone. Instead you spent the entire week holed up in your room or in his office studying geography and architect plans."

"And he's unhappy about that?"

"He's worried that you don't understand the country well enough to build a resort that will fit in with the natural beauty of the land, enhance the flavor, the uniqueness of Argentina—his words, not mine. He says he is a patriot first and a businessman second."

Nicholas paced restlessly around his luxurious office suite on the top floor of the Park Hotel in downtown Pasadena. Pausing at the window, he looked out at the crowded downtown streets and considered his options. Instead of the cars, smog and California sunshine, he saw the beautiful coastline of Argentina, the blue-green sea, pure white sand and unbelievably pink sunsets, a setting that was indelibly printed on his mind. Instinctively his fingers reached into his pocket, curling around the frayed edges of the magazine photograph he couldn't seem to throw away. This was his chance to achieve his lifetime dream.

Juan Carlos's land was perfect for his plans. He would build a five-star hotel resort on one of the most beautiful stretches of coast in the world. It would be his greatest accomplishment, and he wanted that land more than any other piece of property he had bid on. But the clause was ridiculous, absurd. He turned back to Martin with a steely glint in his eyes.

"We've built three resorts in three different countries in the last eight years," he stated. "Every one of them was designed to fit in with the ambience of the setting. Juan Carlos knows that. When I showed him the plans for this resort, he agreed to everything I said."

"But this resort is bigger than the earlier ones, at least twice the size."

"Bigger yes, but in terms of quality, better."

"He's having second thoughts," Martin replied. "The day after you left he took me down to the beach site, and he was very emotional. He talked about the first time he had ever walked on the beach with a woman, the first time he had seen the sunset. I don't think he wants to sell the land at all, but the reality of the situation is that he needs the money and he knows that the local economy would benefit greatly from having a resort there."

"Exactly, which is why he has to sell to us."

"I'm afraid that's going to take some fancy footwork on your part," Martin said with a smile.

"I am not going to learn the tango."

"There's a dance studio in Pasadena, just a few minutes from here."

"Forget it."

"They teach the Argentine tango. In fact the owner was once married to an Argentine businessman. It's the perfect place for you to go."

"Maybe you should offer him more money," Nicholas said pointedly. "We can go a little higher.

That should get rid of the last remaining emotional-ism on his part."

"He doesn't want more money. He wants under-standing, a meeting of the mind, of the soul."

"What on earth are you talking about?"

"Feelings. Something you claim not to have."

"There's no place for emotion in business, not if you want to get ahead."

"You are ahead," Martin reminded him gently. "Further ahead than you ever dreamed you would be. Maybe Juan Carlos is right. Maybe it's time to take a step back, see if you've missed anything along the way."

Missed anything? Nicholas shook his head, think-ing back to the past. He had missed plenty in his life. His early years as an unwanted orphan had been filled with loneliness and pain, but that was in the past. Hard work and single-minded determination had helped him climb out of a long, deep hole, and he was never going back. He was going to have everything he had ever wanted. "When you take a step back, you lose," he said flatly. "The advantage is gone."

"You have exactly three weeks to learn this dance," Martin continued, ignoring his comment. "Juan Carlos has invited us to come to his home then. He'll sign the deed over after your performance."

"And just who am I supposed to dance this tango with? Don't I need a partner?"

"It's too bad you broke up with Karen. She had some nice moves."

"Very nice and all extremely calculated."

"She wasn't so bad."

"Not if you like sharks."

Martin rolled his eyes. "Okay, Karen was a little ambitious. But I'm not sure you'd trust anyone."

"You're probably right. But I don't have time for women right now, anyway. I'm building a business."

"Well, as far as the tango goes, if you can't supply your own partner, Juan Carlos will provide one for you."

"The old man has thought of everything, hasn't he?"

"It sure looks that way. What's the big deal? It's a dance. You've had to do more than this to get what you want. Why balk now?"

"Because I don't dance."

"So you can learn."

"I don't want to learn," Nicholas snapped, feeling as childish as his statement.

"I don't think you have a choice." Martin yawned and stretched as he got to his feet. "Think it over and let me know what you decide. But I think your best bet is to take some lessons during the next three weeks, do the dance and get the contract signed. You need that land. There just isn't anything else suitable."

"There has to be another solution."

"Let me know if you think of one." He reached into his pocket for a business card. "Here's the name of the dance school I was telling you about."

"I am not going to any dance school."

Martin smiled knowingly as he walked to the door. "Ask for Angelia. I hear she dances the tango like no one else."

Angelia Martinez tapped her foot restlessly against the hardwood floor. The beat of the music was flowing through her soul, and she yearned to move into dance and feel the freedom of expression that was so much a part of her. But instead she stared resolutely at the three couples in front of her, each stumbling through their own variation of the waltz.

"They're not exactly Astaire and Rogers, are they?" Ricardo Domingo muttered under his breath as he joined her in front of the barre.

"They're trying," she whispered warningly, smiling at the tortured look on one of the men's faces. "One-two-three, one-two-three," she called out encouragingly. "Listen to the music, let it be your guide." She tapped a wooden cane against the floor, wishing she could pound the rhythm into them.

"Where's your mother?"

"Having lunch with her new boyfriend—why?"

"There's a man out front."

"Can't you help him?"

"Apparently not. He wants to speak to the owner of the school."

"Does he look like a tax collector?"

"No, he looks like an unwilling customer. You know the type."

"All too well, I'm afraid."

"Here's his card. I'll take over for you until you get back."

Angelia looked down at the foil-embossed business card. "Nicholas Hunter, President, HRI, Hunter Resorts International. Sounds impressive, but I've never heard of him."

"That's because you spend all your time in the studio. Nicholas Hunter is a very successful businessman. He builds hotels all over the world."

"And he wants to learn how to dance?"

"I didn't get the details. I just know that he's one student we can't afford to turn down, not if you want to build this studio into a full-scale dance center."

"You're right," she admitted. "Is he alone or with someone?"

"Alone and, judging from his expression, not very happy. He's all yours."

"Thanks a lot." She handed him the cane as the music came to an end. "Run them through the steps one more time and then call it a day. I'll be back as soon as I can."

"No problem. Take your time."

Angelia took a quick glance in the mirror as she slipped out of the studio. Her rose-colored leotards and wraparound skirt were fairly neat, although her face was still somewhat flushed from an earlier aerobics class and her long black hair was drifting out of its single braid in curling tendrils. Tucking a few pieces of hair behind her ear, she shrugged. She was a dance teacher. That was what she looked like.

Her first glimpse of Nicholas Hunter made her wish she had taken the time to change or at least comb her hair. He was standing in front of their showcase, staring at the photographs of their last dance recital. She opened her mouth to call to him, but the harsh expression on his face made her pause, and she studied him for a moment.

He was dressed in a navy blue suit with a white button-down shirt and a silk tie. He was very well put together, with dark brown hair that just touched the collar of his crisp white shirt. His profile was strong and defined, not handsome but intriguing. Then he turned, and his bright blue eyes caught her by surprise, for the color seemed at odds with his otherwise somber appearance.

"Miss Martinez?" he questioned.

"Angelia," she corrected, walking forward to join him. "And you are Nicholas Hunter?"

"Yes." he gave her hand a brief shake and then stepped back, shoving his hands into his pockets in a gesture that reminded her fondly of her younger brother, Michael, when he was feeling embarrassed about something.

"Can I help you?"

"I need tango lessons."

Her dark brown eyes widened in surprise. "Tango lessons?" A sexy passionate dance for this conservative businessman?

"Yes, as soon as possible."

"I see. Do you have a partner that will be joining you?"

"No."

"Then the lessons are just for yourself?"

"Yes."

His short answers were a disappointment. She was getting tired of teaching people who had no real desire to dance but for reasons of their own had to learn. Nicholas Hunter obviously fit into that category.

With a sigh she turned aside, stepping behind the counter of the front desk and reaching for their brochure of class information. "We have a tango class starting tomorrow night, and there are two women who still need a partner."

"No. I want private lessons. Just two or three to learn the basics. That's it."

"Why?" she asked abruptly, forgetting her usual diplomatic questions.

Nicholas stared back at her, a mixture of anger and unease in his eyes. "Does it matter?"

"I think so. I like to get to know my students to understand what they hope to get out of their dance instruction."

"I just want to learn the damn tango," he snapped. "Look, this isn't my idea. It's just something that I have to do. Can you help me or not?"

"I can help you," she said slowly, wondering if she was making the right decision. She had taught unwilling students before, but they had usually been married or at least attached to a willing partner. Nicholas Hunter's back was so stiff, his face so rigid, she couldn't imagine him dancing the tango, a passionate, earthy dance that could only be done well without inhibition, without restraint. Getting him to unbend would certainly be a challenge, a very attractive challenge.

"Good," he said abruptly, interrupting her reverie. "When do we begin?"

"You can start tomorrow evening," she said hastily, putting a short rein on her wayward thoughts. "I'd like you to come early, though, about six-thirty. I want you to see the tango demonstration that Ricardo and I will be putting on for the group class. It will be easier to teach you the steps if you have a good idea of what the dance is supposed to look like."

"Fine. Is there anything special I should bring?"

"Comfortable clothing and perhaps a smile?"

For a moment his lips started to curve, but then he thought better of it. "I'll be here at six-thirty. Do you want a deposit for the class?"

"No, I think I can trust you."

He shook his head, an oblique expression flitting through his eyes. Then he pulled out his checkbook and wrote her a check. "This should cover something. Let me know what the balance is."

She nodded and accepted the check as he turned to leave. She wanted to call him back, to ask him why he needed to learn the tango, why he couldn't smile and why he didn't want to be trusted. But she remained silent. Tomorrow she would teach him how to tango, a dance that had a way of stripping away secrets and exposing the heart.

"Why are you taking on more customers when I'm planning to close down the school?" Michelle Danielson demanded, pacing back and forth in front of the barre as Angelia stretched her long slender legs in preparation for her dance demonstration later that evening.

"Because I'm not going to let you close the school, Mother," she replied, continuing the argument that had started the day before when she had signed Nicholas up for tango lessons. She caught her mother's eye in the mirror and smiled persuasively. "I want to keep the school going."

"But you don't have to do this anymore. I'm going to marry Howard, and of course you and Michael will come to live with us and share in everything that we have. Howard is a very wealthy man. He wants to support us, all of us. Our struggling days are over."

Angelia squared her shoulders and counted to ten. "If you want to marry Howard Bellerman, that's fine. But I'm twenty-six years old and I have my own life now. I want to turn this school into a thriving dance center. I'd like to see us offer more classes of all different types and make our lessons available to some of the less-privileged kids. I want to stretch beyond the basic ballroom dancing and ballet. There's so much we can do. We haven't even begun to tap into the talent that we see here every day.''

"Talent? What are you talking about? Most of the students here are bored housewives or children. They're not serious dancers.''

"I think we can draw the serious dancers. Ricardo is a fantastic instructor and choreographer, and Agnes is wonderful with ballet and I fancy myself a fairly talented Latin dancer, not to mention your reputation.''

"You don't have to flatter me. My reputation, such as it is, was earned a long time ago. I doubt many of the students even remember my brief career. But I really think you're fighting a losing battle. Our customers are just too run-of-the-mill. They're not special enough.''

"Nicholas Hunter is definitely not run-of-the-mill,'' she said, wishing she had kept silent when she saw the speculation in her mother's eyes.

"Nicholas Hunter—the businessman that I keep hearing about? The one who built the fancy Park Hotel downtown?''

"Yes. He's my new student, the one you didn't want me to take.''

"What on earth is someone like that doing here?''

"He wants to learn the tango.''

"Why?''

Angelia smiled for the first time. "I have no idea. But if he wants to learn the dance, I'm more than happy to teach him.''

"He's single, you know, and very rich.''

"Good for him."

"Oh, Angelia, why don't you ever consider your future?"

"I am considering my future."

"Teaching dance in a small Pasadena dance school is not much of a future. I want more for you, for all of us."

"But that's what you want, not what I want," Angelia said gently. Her brown eyes softened at her mother's worried face. She knew there were lines underneath the expertly applied makeup, indelible signs of stress from the past fifteen years. It wasn't surprising that she didn't want to fight anymore. But she wasn't ready to give up her dreams, not yet. "I like to teach dance. I like to perform, but I also like to watch others experience the joy of their own movements. It's a great feeling."

"Most of the students here trip over their own two feet," Michelle argued. "We don't have any soaring eagles, just a lot of ducks."

Angelia burst out laughing at her mother's disgruntled expression. "Ducks can turn into swans."

"Not in real-life, sweetheart. I just want what's best for you," Michelle continued. "I hate to see you bury yourself in this school when you have other options."

"I'm not interested in finding a husband."

"You should be. It's not natural to live life alone."

"I suppose that's why you've had two already," she said tartly.

Michelle sent her a hurt look. "I made a few mistakes in my life, but at least I go on trying."

Angelia sighed. "I'm sorry. But are you sure about Howard? Do you really think he's the right man for you? David didn't work out, and he's certainly nothing like—"

"Your father?" Michelle finished bitterly. "It always comes back to him, doesn't it? Why can't you just forget him?"

"Forget my father? How could I do that?"

"He forgot us."

"Did he? Sometimes I wonder."

"You wonder?" Michelle repeated incredulously. "You wonder about a man that you haven't heard from in almost eighteen years, a man that never sent one penny toward your support?"

The accusation hung between them like a thick curtain. What could she say when every word that had come out of her mother's mouth was the absolute truth? After a long moment she shrugged her shoulders. "I don't want to get into this with you, not right now. My class will be here in a few minutes."

Michelle hesitated and then nodded her head. "Fine. Where is your brother? I want to tell him my good news."

"Probably at work. I think he's working the dinner shift tonight."

"Again? Michael works too hard for a seventeen-year-old boy. I know he'll be pleased with this marriage. After high school he can go straight to college and then law school without having to clean up after those snooty customers at Dalmonico's."

Angelia rolled her eyes at the familiar theme. Swinging her leg off the barre, she straightened and stretched her arms over her head. "Are you staying for my tango class?"

"No, I don't care to see you dance the tango. Too many memories. I'm going to dinner. I'll have to talk to Howard about the school again. He wants us to travel and he doesn't want me to be tied down with the school.''

"But won't you miss it?" Angelia asked curiously. "I know you've never really liked to teach, but you're a wonderful dancer. You make things look so easy, so smooth, especially when you're just dancing for yourself. I've seen you a few times when the school is closed, and you think you're alone. You have more talent in your little finger than I have in my whole body."

Michelle dropped her eyes in embarrassment. "I wish I'd known you were watching."

"Why? I love to watch you. I just wish you'd do it more often."

"I do love to dance," Michelle admitted slowly. "For a long time I didn't want to, it hurt too much. But now I can't seem to stop myself. It just bursts out of me, especially since I met Howard. He makes me feel like dancing again."

"I'm glad." Angelia smiled. "So why do you want to close down the school?"

"Because I don't want to teach anymore. It frustrates me."

"Then don't teach. I can run things here, and eventually I hope I can buy you out completely. I know I can make a success of this. I really want to."

"Oh, Angelia. I only started the school to support us until we got on our feet. I never intended for you to spend your life teaching dance. I want so much more for you."

"But I like what I'm doing. I'm not the kind of person to settle for a nine-to-five job in a stuffy office. I like variety, freedom, flexibility, and I've always loved coming here. When I'm dancing it reminds me of—Argentina.''

"And why would you want to be reminded of a place that brought us so much pain?" Michelle shook her head in bewilderment. "You're so like your father. I don't think I've ever understood either one of you."

"Sometimes I don't understand myself. I just know that I feel a need to keep in touch with that part of my soul."

"We need to talk," Michelle said, her voice rising sharply. "There are things you should know, things I should have told you about the past."

Angelia's smile faded, a feeling of uneasiness spreading through her. "What haven't you told me?"

"Just little things," Michelle said nervously. "They're probably not important. I just don't like to see you romanticize your father and our life in Argentina."

"Then tell me the truth."

"I will, but not tonight. I have to meet Howard, and you have to meet—Nicholas Hunter. That should be interesting."

Angelia smiled, pushing the problems of the past out of her mind. Her mother was right for once. She was looking forward to the evening, to her new challenge.

"Do you think he really wants to dance?" Michelle asked curiously.

"I'm not sure what his motives are. I just know that I'm going to have to dance the tango in such a way that he won't be able to resist the urge to join me."

Chapter Two

Nicholas took a deep breath and shifted position, trying to appear as unaffected by the dance as everyone else in the room. But the truth was that Angelia's version of the tango was like nothing he had ever seen before. Her black silk dress swirled around long shapely legs as she spun and kicked and dipped with a sultry abandon that made his head spin and his heart beat faster. He was dismayed and exhilarated at the same time, wondering how on earth he was going to perform this dance in front of Juan Carlos.

Trying to remember his original motives, he forced himself to focus on the technical steps of the dance, studying Ricardo's moves as well as Angelia's. But it was difficult to concentrate. The heady beat of the music was filling him with strange emotions, feelings that he didn't like to acknowledge. For a split second he was tempted to walk—make that run—to the nearest exit. It had been a long time since he had run away from anything.

The music ended with a flourish, and amid the clapping and excited comments, he felt the tension ease out of his shoulders. The tango was just a dance. He was reading too much into it, making it more than it was. While the others were talking, he slipped into the hallway and made his way over to the drinking fountain.

The cool water was brisk and refreshing, and he felt more in control by the time he went back into the studio. He watched the final few minutes of the group class, taking pleasure in the fact that no one else seemed to know the steps and the bumbling attempts he now saw were a far cry from the demonstration he had just witnessed.

When the class was over, Angelia walked over to him, her cheeks red, her dark eyes sparkling with excitement. She had a warm, open face, filled with emotion and caring and a zest for life that touched a chord deep within him. He felt his misgivings return.

"What did you think?" she asked curiously.

"It was nice."

Angelia laughed at his inadequate description. "Don't worry. We'll start slow and take it one step at a time. I know the dance can be overwhelming, but once you get started, I think you'll do fine."

"Maybe we should wait until everyone is gone."

"We can go next door. The classes tend to linger for a while. Follow me."

She led the way into the next room, which was a smaller version of the main studio but still replete with a mirror and a barre. She walked over and pushed a tape into the tape recorder and then smiled at him as music filled the room.

He was standing self-consciously in the middle of the floor with his arms crossed protectively in front of him. He looked more human than he had the day before, having exchanged his sophisticated business suit for a pair of faded blue jeans, white chambray shirt and tennis shoes. But his scowl was still planted firmly across his face.

"The music just makes you want to dance, doesn't it?"

"Not really," he muttered as she walked over to join him.

"I promise this won't hurt a bit."

"That's what my dentist always says before he stabs me with a needle."

She extended her hands, palm open. "I'm unarmed."

"Let's just get this over with."

"Okay. Let me show you some of the basic positions." She took his hands and placed one around her waist and then stretched the other out in front of them. "Are you comfortable?"

He swallowed and nodded tightly. "Fine."

She smiled to herself and then began to count out the first combination of steps. "One-two-three-four—ouch." She pulled her foot out from under his.

"Sorry."

"No problem. I forgot to tell you that tennis shoes don't work well on the floor. Why don't you take them off."

"Take them off," he echoed. "Do I really have to do that?"

"Unless you want to trip over your toes for the next hour."

His mouth puckered into another frown as he kicked off his shoes and revealed a pair of mismatched socks, one white, the other a pale peach. Angelia bit back a smile. "That's better. Now, let's try it again."

She prodded him to move, pushing her body against his so that he could feel the way she was leading. They made it halfway across the floor before he pulled away, scowling down at her. "Do we have to be so close together?"

"This isn't a solo dance, Mr. Hunter."

"But isn't the man supposed to lead?"

"Once he knows how, it usually works that way," she admitted, stifling a grin at his discomfiture.

"Then let's do it that way. Just tell me what you want me to do. I can take it from there."

"All right. I want you to lead me across the room. I want us to not walk but slide—effortlessly. Then we make the turn sharply and with pizzazz."

"Pizzazz?" he asked dazedly.

"The tango is a dance of passion, excitement. Every movement is pointed and sharp." She took his hand and twirled her body into his, coming to rest with her hands on his chest, the tip of her head just touching his chin. His heartbeat quickened beneath her palm, his breath hitting her cheek as she stared up at him. Then she pushed off, spinning out in the same manner.

His eyes turned an even deeper shade of blue as he stared at her. "I don't think I can do this," he said gruffly.

"You can do it," she encouraged, trying to ignore the sudden tightness in her chest. "You just have to try to stay loose, be ready for the unexpected."

"I don't like the unexpected. Why don't you tell me what you're going to do before you do it. Then I'll be ready."

"That takes some of the fun out of the dance, but if that's the way you like it . . ."

"It is."

Her lips turned into an inviting smile. "Then let's dance."

They made it halfway across the room before Nicholas tripped. He pulled back and frowned at her.

"Don't worry about it. Let's just keep going."

He sighed and placed his hands stiffly on her body. He tried to follow her counts, but his feet seemed too big next to hers, his movements awkward and clumsy next to her warm, swaying body. He tried to relax, but memories of past dance lessons began to come back to him. He couldn't do it. He was uncoordinated and clumsy, and within minutes she would be looking at him like everyone else had done—with pity.

"That's it," he announced abruptly, dropping his hands so suddenly, Angelia almost slipped.

"But we've only just begun," she protested. "Did I do something wrong?"

"You?" he questioned in confusion. "No, it's me. I can't do it. I can't dance." He shook his head and walked briskly over to the other side of the room where he began putting on his tennis shoes. "I'm sorry to have taken up your time. Of course, I'll pay you for the full hour and anything else that you require."

"That won't be necessary. I really think you should give yourself a little more time to catch on. Learning the tango is not an easy feat."

"Especially for my feet," he added. "It's been a long day, and it's too hot in here." He pulled at the collar of his shirt. "I need some air."

"There's an outdoor patio just through those doors," she said with quiet amusement.

"Good." He walked quickly over to the French doors and stepped out onto the darkened patio.

Angelia hesitated and then followed him outside. She wrapped her arms round her waist as the brisk night air hit her face. It was chilly but refreshing. She walked over to the balcony, and looked out past the darkened residential neighborhoods of Pasadena to the brightly lit downtown area.

"I love this time of the night," she said after a while. "The view is so peaceful, so lovely. And it's quiet. You can't hear the traffic anymore, just the crickets and the sounds of the night." She smiled up at him. "I've never gotten used to living in a big city, I'm afraid."

He looked at her in bemusement, feeling as out of depth on the starlit patio as he had in the dance studio. "Where are you from?"

"Argentina, a town called Necochea. I was born there. I still miss it."

"When did you leave?"

She smiled wistfully. "A long time ago. I was eight years old when my mother and I came to the United States. I've never been able to go back."

"Oh."

Normally she would have explained why, but his short answer made her hesitate. He was clearly uncomfortable with the whole situation, and once again she wondered why he was here, why he said he wanted tango lessons when it was clear he hated to dance.

"Why are you here?" she asked abruptly, struck by the conflicting emotions she saw in his eyes.

"I have to learn the tango."

"But why? I know you're not enjoying this."

Nicholas sighed and turned to face her inquisitive dark eyes. "Because it's part of a business deal."

"A business deal? I don't understand."

"Neither do I. In fact I'm beginning to realize just how ridiculous this whole idea is."

"I don't understand what the tango has to do with business."

"It shouldn't have anything to do with it," he agreed. After a long pause he offered her a short explanation. "I want to buy some land in Argentina. The man who owns the land in question is very eccentric. He wants me to dance the tango to prove I understand their culture."

She looked at him in amazement, a smile dawning on her face as she began to understand the situation. "You have to dance the tango to make a deal? What a great idea."

His jaw tightened, and his eyes turned dark as he sent her a frosty look. "Are you kidding? It's a damn inconvenience."

"But a great opportunity for you to learn something new."

"Yeah, and it's good for your business, too."

"Not if you're going to give up after fifteen minutes," she challenged. "Where's your sense of adventure, your spirit?"

"I'm a businessman, Miss Martinez. Adding up the balance sheet is enough excitement for me."

She heard the finality in his tone, the harshness of his words, but for some reason she didn't quite believe him. On the surface he appeared to be a serious, conservative businessman, but she was beginning to sense undercurrents of emotion from the frustration in his voice and the restless drumming of his fingers against the railing. For a man who seemed to have so much, he didn't appear to be very happy.

"What are you thinking?" he asked, cutting into her speculative stare.

She pursed her lips and considered the question. "That I have my work cut out for me. I thought ten-year-old Jeremy Hudson was going to be my worst student, but I was wrong."

He scowled, but under her teasing smile, the frown gradually turned into a twisted grin. "I know I shouldn't ask, but what does Jeremy Hudson do?"

"He trips the girls on purpose, and when they turn around he yanks their skirts down to their knees."

"Nice guy. But I'm pretty good at tripping myself. That's why this isn't going to work."

"I think it can, if you're willing to try. You just have to loosen up a little. You seem to be naturally coordinated and athletic, dancing shouldn't be a problem for you." She rested her arms on the railing and stared out at the view. "Of course, it's your decision. It does take a certain amount of guts to dance."

"I know what you're trying to do," Nicholas said. "And I don't take dares."

"Whatever you say."

Angelia fell silent as the air crackled between them with an unspoken challenge.

"I have to admit that you make it look incredibly easy," Nicholas said finally. "The way you danced with Ricardo was something else." He cleared his throat as his voice caught on his words.

"Ricardo always makes me look good. That's part of his job."

"Now you're being modest."

She laughed. "Okay, I'm great, I admit it. But tonight everything really clicked. Sometimes it works like that. But it takes a special connection between the dancers. Ricardo and I are friends, long-standing friends. We understand each other, we know our strengths and our weaknesses and we play on them. That's why we tango so well together. But each partner, each team of tango dancers is different. When you and I dance..." Her words drifted away under the sudden intensity in his blue eyes.

"What were you going to say?"

She hesitated, remembering those brief moments in his arms. Despite his awkwardness, his restraint, she had sensed something between them, a chemistry that sent a tingle down her spine every time they touched.

"Angelia," he said, his eyes seeking, questioning.

The breeze blew her hair in front of her eyes, masking the sudden flare of emotion, and the moment passed. "Just that you and I would dance the tango differently than Ricardo and I did," she muttered.

"I'm sure we would. But I don't think I want to find out."

"It's not that bad. You don't have much experience with dancing, do you?"

He made a face, remembering the short-lived dance classes of his teenage years when the Sisters at the convent had tried to prepare him to enter public high school. They had wanted him to fit in, to make the transition easily, but in their naïveté they had only made him feel humiliated. The thought of dancing again made him feel sick.

"Did I hit a nerve?" Angelia asked softly.

"No, I was just trying to remember when I last danced."

"I would think in your social circle that you would do a lot of dancing."

"When the music starts, I usually claim a sprained ankle, a pulled hamstring or a bad knee."

"But why? Dancing is fun."

"More like torture."

His dramatic sigh made her smile. "I've never had a martyr for a student before."

His lips turned upward involuntarily, the smile slowly spreading across his face. "You're a tough teacher."

"I think you can handle it. Can you come again tomorrow night?"

"I don't know. I'll have to check my schedule."

"Yeah. Maybe you'll have a dentist appointment instead."

"Angelia," a voice called, breaking into their conversation. The studio door opened, sending a shaft of bright light onto the patio. "Angelia, are you out here?"

"Yes," she answered as her mother walked out to join them.

"I'm glad I caught you, I wanted to tell you my news." Michelle paused, looking from one to the other. "I'm sorry, I didn't mean to interrupt."

"This is Nicholas Hunter. My mother, Michelle Danielson," Angelia introduced, watching them shake hands.

"Mr. Hunter, I'm so pleased to meet you. I've heard a lot about you and I must say your new downtown hotel is quite spectacular."

"Thank you. We wanted it to be one of a kind."

"I understand that Angelia is going to teach you the tango."

"Possibly," he conceded.

"Well, she's the best, even if she is my daughter."

"What did you want to tell me?" Angelia interrupted.

"Howard and I have set the date, a week from Saturday, in honor of Valentine's Day." She held out her hand to show off a big, flashy diamond. "Isn't it beautiful?"

"Gorgeous."

"I know. It's everything I hoped for. I can't believe it's really happening to me. I'm so happy. I know this one is going to be the right one."

"I hope so, Mom."

"I'm sorry. I'm interrupting your conversation."

"No, we were just taking a break."

Michelle smiled speculatively and then nodded her head. "I can talk to you tomorrow. We can go over all the details then. Why don't you call me or stop by before you come to the studio?"

"It will have to be before eight, I have a class at nine tomorrow."

"That's much too early. Perhaps lunch would be better. I'll meet you at noon at Lombardi's. It's right next door to Neiman Marcus. Maybe we can stop by the store after we eat and look at some dresses."

Angelia rolled her eyes as her mother's excitement began to escalate. "We'll talk about it tomorrow. Congratulations."

"Thank you, dear." Michelle leaned over and kissed her on the cheek. "Good night. Good luck with your lessons, Mr. Hunter."

Nicholas smiled a thank-you as she left, closing the door behind her and once more shrouding the tiny patio in privacy.

"You must be very happy for your mother."

"I suppose so," she said hesitantly. "This will be her third marriage."

"Three marriages? Incredible."

"She made a few mistakes, but I think this one should work out. At least I hope so."

Nicholas shook his head, making Angelia feel as if she should apologize for her mother's behavior. But that was ridiculous. Her mother's marriages had nothing to do with him. "I suppose your parents have been married to each other forever."

"I don't have any parents."

The bitterness in his tone felt like a kick in the stomach. "I'm sorry."

He shrugged. "I think I'll call it a night."

"I should go, too. It's late, and I have to close up the school."

He turned to leave, and instinctively she put a hand on his arm, feeling a sudden need to clear the air before he left. "I really am sorry about that remark. I have a tendency to speak before I think."

His face softened for a second, but his eyes were still shuttered. "Forget it."

"What about tomorrow?" she asked as they walked back into the studio.

"I'll call you."

"Lights out, folks," Ricardo said, stepping into the hallway from one of the smaller studios. "Are you done? I'm closing up."

"We're done," Nicholas replied firmly. "Good night, Angelia. Ricardo."

"Good night," she muttered under her breath, turning her back on Ricardo's inquisitive eyes and her own crazy thoughts. She didn't want to answer any questions about Nicholas Hunter, mainly because she didn't have any answers. So she waved Ricardo on and set about locking up the school for the night.

"Angelia, Angelia? Are you there?" Michelle's fingers snapped in front of her face.

"I'm sorry. What did you say?"

"I said if you're done twirling your salad around on your fork, we might as well pay the check and stop by the dress salon next door."

"I'm not very hungry today."

"Can I guess why?"

"No," she said shortly, reaching for the check.

"It has something to do with Nicholas Hunter and that intimate little scene I broke up last night."

"It was hardly intimate. We were just talking and getting some fresh air."

"But there's something about that man that bothers you, isn't there?" Michelle prodded. "Admit it, you're interested."

"The only thing I am interested in is teaching Nicholas Hunter how to tango."

"Don't be silly. The man is positively gorgeous. I can't imagine what you're looking for."

"I'm not looking, Mother, that's the point." She glanced down at her watch. "We should get going. I only have about twenty minutes to spare. I have some kids from the Family Shelter coming in for a movement class this afternoon."

"More free lessons?" her mother protested, momentarily sidetracked. "We can't afford that."

"It's just an hour, and I like to do it. It's nothing for you to worry about."

"I can't help worrying about you."

Angelia sighed. "I thought we were talking about the school."

"The school, you, your brother, me," her mother tossed out in agitation. "I can't marry Howard with all these problems weighing on my mind."

Angelia rolled her eyes in exasperation. "You're going to marry Howard and everyone else is going to be just fine."

"I don't worry so much about Michael. He's nearly grown now, and he and Howard get along so well. But you—"

"I can take care of myself," she interrupted. "I certainly don't need a man to do it for me. That's the most outdated notion I've ever heard."

"Maybe for you, but I know how hard it is to make it in this world when you're a woman alone. You should be thinking about marriage and family, not about running a dance school."

Angelia silently counted to ten. "Marriage and family is the last thing I want to worry about."

"Because of me? I've soured you, haven't I?" Michelle's green eyes flashed with guilt. "I tried not to. I know I made mistakes, but it wasn't my fault."

"I'm not blaming you for anything. But I've seen firsthand that marriage and happily-ever-after are just a myth."

"Not for the right two people. Your father and I were just too different. We didn't understand each other, and I couldn't live with him."

"What about David?"

"Another mistake," she dismissed. "But I know Howard and I are going to make it. This time it's going to work."

Angelia softened at her mother's worried expression. "I hope so for your sake. Speaking of which, we better go take a look at those dresses. What color do you want this time?"

"I thought maybe a peach," Michelle replied with relief etched in her tone. "I'd love to see you in something vibrant and colorful to go with your big brown eyes. Do you think Michael will wear a tuxedo again?"

"He'll grumble, but I'm sure he'll do it for you. You know he can't bear to see you unhappy, and neither can I."

"And that's how I feel about both of you," Michelle said forcefully, jumping back to her original topic. "I want you to be happy, Angelia, but besides just having a nice, easy life, I want you to feel the excitement of love. Don't turn your back on that because of my mistakes."

"I'll try not to," she replied, knowing in her heart how difficult it would be to keep that promise.

Chapter Three

"Bad news, Angelia."

Ricardo's somber greeting made her pause as she walked into the dance studio forty-five minutes later.

"What happened?"

"A pipe burst over the main studio. Water poured through the ceiling. By the time we got the main valve shut off, everything was ruined."

"No." Her whispered denial was met with a shake of his head. "Tell me you're kidding."

"I'm sorry. I know this is going to set you back. The problem is this is an old building. It needs to be completely checked out. When your mother bought it ten years ago, she knew there were problems, she just didn't want to do anything about them."

"We never had any extra money," she defended. "We just tried to keep the basics covered. How bad are the smaller studios?"

"Studio A was flooded. B wasn't so bad, but the real problem is the hardwood floors. Repairing the buckling is going to take time, and we won't be able to use them while they're being repaired. Agnes is already calling around to cancel today's classes."

Angelia followed him down the hallway and into the main studio, staring in horror at the yellowing walls and two of her staff members trying to soak up the pool of water with towels and mops.

"Damn. This is the last thing we needed. Where are the kids from the Family Shelter?"

"I sent them back. I told them that as soon as we get back on our feet, we'll run the movement classes."

"They must have been really disappointed."

"Yeah, but I think you have more pressing problems than those kids to worry about. What are we going to do?"

"I don't know," she said quietly, her heart sinking with the weight of reality. Their savings would be stretched to the limit with this new disaster, and once they started opening up the walls, who knew what other horrors would be discovered.

"Are you going to call your mother?" Ricardo asked curiously.

"Eventually," she muttered. "But this will only give her more ammunition to close the school down."

"Maybe she's right. You can work for someone else. Los Angeles is a big market, and of course you could always go to New York."

She looked at him in surprise. "I'm not interested in going to New York, and downtown Pasadena is a big enough city for me."

"Most dancers wouldn't agree with you, especially ones with ambition."

"I have ambitions, but they're not so big I have to change my whole life-style. This place is more than just a dance school to me. It's like home."

Ricardo smiled, putting an arm around her shoulders and giving her a hug. "I know your heart and soul is tied up in this studio. I don't know why, but..."

"It's a long story."

"I'm just not sure you can fight your way out of this one or if you should even try. You're a dancer, Angelia."

"And a businesswoman," she added, ignoring his look of disbelief. "It's true. I can be serious when I have to be."

"But you don't have to be. That's the point."

"I'll just have to find a way to pay for the repairs."

"How are you going to do that? You don't have any money."

"No, but I have a lot of imagination. There has to be a way to raise some extra cash. Maybe a fund-raiser or a dance exhibition," she tossed out optimistically. "I'm sure we can think of something."

"It's a long shot. What about a bank loan?"

She made a face at his suggestion. "Bankers don't seem to look kindly on lowly dance schools that rarely show a profit. I don't know. Maybe we could get something, but it's probably going to take a while. Right now we need to get this room cleaned up and try to find an alternative site for our classes. If we can keep those going, we won't have to refund a lot of our tuition money.

"What about insurance?"

"Don't ask. I know we have something, but it's not much."

Ricardo nodded in commiseration. "I better help Agnes with the phone calls."

"Thanks. Try to keep everyone's spirits up, and I'll sit down with my bank book and try to figure out where we stand financially."

"Don't let your pride get in the way," Ricardo warned. "If Howard Bellerman or anyone else wants to be a patron to the arts, let them."

"I don't want to call Howard on this. He's marrying my mother, not me."

"What about Nicholas Hunter?"

She immediately shook her head at the suggestion. "I don't think so."

"Why not? He's a student here, he has a lot of money and could probably use a nice tax deduction. Maybe you should ask him if he's interested in helping."

"Nicholas Hunter hates dance. He's only learning the tango to seal a business deal."

"No kidding?" Ricardo asked with interest.

"Needless to say, he's not here of his own free will."

"Maybe not at first, but the two of you looked pretty cozy last night."

"We were talking. He's an interesting man."

"Interesting, huh?"

"Stop it, Ricardo. I just went through this conversation with my mother. I'm not doing it again."

"Just trying to take your mind off your problems. I'll go make those calls. Then I better call my father and beg for a loan. I have a feeling our salaries are going to get pretty tight in the next few weeks."

"I hope we won't have to cut back," she replied with a frown. "I don't want to lose you or Agnes or anyone else, for that matter."

"We're not going anywhere. I just hope your optimism isn't misplaced this time."

"It isn't." She forced a smile. "Don't worry about all this. Everything is going to be all right. I'll make it work."

Nicholas paced restlessly around the living room, stopping to take a swig of beer as he checked the clock.

"It's five minutes to seven," Martin interjected. "Three minutes later than the last time you looked. What's with you anyway?"

"I'd just like to get this tango lesson over with," he replied. "For two cents I would have canceled the whole thing."

"We're not talking about two cents here, Nick. This is a very big deal for the company."

"I want out of this tango, Martin."

"There's no other way."

"I want you to find one. Talk to Steven Bruni. See if we can't find a way to circumvent this legally."

"Bruni is a lawyer, not a magician. There's nothing illegal about the terms."

"Talk to him anyway," he yelled in frustration. "I know you think this is very funny, but you're not the one who has to stand up and make a fool of himself."

"I doubt you'll do that. Have you found yourself a partner yet?"

"No, because I don't intend to go through with this."

"Better start thinking. You can't just ask some woman at the last minute. You need to get someone involved right now, so they can learn with you."

"I can't think of one woman who would be willing to do this with me."

"You can't? I can think of about a hundred. You're not trying very hard."

Nicholas shook his head and frowned. Ever since he had left Angelia's studio the evening before, he had been looking for a reason to quit, a way out, but as Martin said, there wasn't one. If he wanted that land, he was going to have to learn the tango, and Angelia was probably the best teacher he could find. In fact he couldn't imagine dancing the tango with anyone else.

When they had started to dance, he found himself wanting to touch her, to hold her close, to sweep her into his arms in the same possessive, sensual manner that Ricardo had. But instead he had bumbled and stepped on her feet. That was reality, his reality.

Damn. He had to stop thinking about her. He needed to keep his distance, so why was he about to spend another hour with her in the intimacy of his home?

"I didn't want her to come to the house," he said suddenly, voicing his thoughts aloud. "But she had some crisis at the studio, and it was here or not at all. I tried to cancel, but that woman is stubborn, won't take no for an answer."

Martin shrugged, glancing around the large sunken living room. "You've got plenty of room here. What's the problem?"

Nicholas sighed, unable to express his uneasiness about inviting Angelia into his home, but the doorbell rang and it was too late to change his mind.

Martin jumped to his feet. "I'll get it." He threw open the front door and grinned. "Angelia Martinez?"

She smiled in confusion. "Yes. But you're not Nicholas."

"Martin Hennessey," he returned, stepping back.

"Nice to meet you. Hi, Nicholas." She looked past Martin's boyish grin into Nicholas's bright blue eyes and smiled, pleased by the rare flicker of warmth in his eyes.

"Angelia. Did you have any trouble finding us?"

"No, your directions were quite clear. I really love this part of Pasadena."

Martin cleared his throat as their conversation lapsed into a long, steady glance. "Why don't we go into the living room," he suggested.

"Sure," Nicholas said hastily, motioning her toward the large double doors leading off the entry. "It's right in there."

Angelia took a long look around the fashionably decorated living room and thought perhaps she had stepped into the middle of a movie set. Everything was lush and rich, from the grand piano in the corner to the Impressionist paintings on the wall and the oriental carpet covering the sheen of hardwood floors.

"This is incredible," she breathed, looking around her in awe. It was a far cry from her one-bedroom apartment or even memories of her father's large house in Argentina.

"It works," Nicholas replied, taking her sweater and purse and setting them carefully on the love seat. "Would you like a drink or something?"

"No, I'm fine for now."

"So, let's see you two dance," Martin encouraged, holding a beer in one hand as he leaned against the doorjamb. "Don't mind me."

"Out, Martin," Nicholas ordered.

"And miss all the fun? No way."

Angelia smiled. "I don't think you're helping."

"Just think of me as Juan Carlos."

"No, not yet," Nicholas replied firmly. "No audiences until I have a few more lessons."

"You mean Angelia is the only one who gets to see you sweat?"

Nicholas looked into Angelia's warm brown eyes and frowned. "She's the only one."

His irritated look was filled with another, more complicated emotion, and for a moment Angelia was tempted to ask Martin to stay to provide a buffer between them. But apparently he had read Nicholas's look as perceptively as she had.

"I'll be going, then. But you have to promise me a private showing before we leave for Argentina."

"I'll think about it," Nicholas replied, tossing him his jacket. "See you tomorrow."

"Yeah. Good night, Angelia, it was nice meeting you. I hope you can do something with this stiff. We've got a lot of money riding on this deal."

"I think Nicholas is going to surprise you," she said confidently.

"I hope so," he returned, exchanging an enigmatic look with his friend before he walked out of the room.

"Are you sure you don't want a drink, some food?" Nicholas asked abruptly, breaking the silence between them.

"I'm fine. Why don't we start?" She reached for her purse and pulled out a tape. "Let's begin by listening to the music without doing anything. I want you to think about what you're hearing, let your body respond to the music in whatever way you like."

"What do you mean?" he asked cautiously.

"Let yourself sway, tap your foot or move your body. Just relax, let your hair down, so to speak."

He immediately shook his head. "I can't do that. I'd feel silly."

"Why? I'm not going to watch you. In fact I'm going to be doing the same thing." She smiled persuasively. "We're just going to have some fun."

She walked over and inserted the tape into his stereo system and then stood motionlessly in the center of the room. As the soft strains of Latin music began to escalate, she closed her eyes and took a long deep breath. Slowly she began to rotate her head, a dreamy expression coming over her face.

Nicholas watched her with fascination. Her movements were soft and gentle but more seductive than anything he had seen. He found himself wanting to reach out and touch her, to trace the fine bones of her face, to pull the rubber band from her hair and watch the waves tumble freely down around her shoulders. He felt hot, and beads of perspiration began to gather on his forehead. Damn, he was starting to sweat, and they weren't even dancing.

Angelia flicked one eye open and smiled. "You're not feeling the music, Nick. Just relax, tap your foot."

"This is silly."

"Just try," she ordered.

He sighed and shifted position, concentrating his attention on the diagonal pattern of his wood floor and the bright white cushions on the couch, trying to ignore her face and the slender curves of her body outlined by black knit pants and a turquoise T-shirt that was way too small.

Despite his reluctance to dance, his body began to pick up the drumming beat of the music. He shifted his weight again, crossing and uncrossing his arms, and then he began to tap his foot.

Angelia was swaying now, her eyes studying him thoughtfully. After a moment she reached out her hand to him, smiling her encouragement, her unrestricted acceptance of his movements.

He took her hand, stiffly moving into the position she had taught him. They started to dance, slowly and then more surely as he began to follow her lead. He stumbled a few times, but it surprised him how well they seemed to move together. The touch of her legs against his, her breasts against his chest, made the awkwardness disappear from his movements. Staring down into her velvet brown eyes, he felt completely lost to reality. Then the music stopped and the silence broke them apart.

"That was nice," she said softly, stepping away, her dark eyes reflecting the lights from his chandelier.

"It wasn't too bad."

"You might even start to like it."

"Don't push your luck."

She laughed and walked over to rewind the tape. "You're just a big grumbler, Nick. You don't scare me anymore."

"I didn't know that I did," he said, reaching for his half-filled beer.

"A little. You're a rather intimidating person at first glance. And I've never felt comfortable around successful businessmen. I guess it's hard to measure up to all that sophistication when I spend most of my time working out in leotards."

His lips curved into a small smile. "That's funny. Because when I first saw you, you scared the hell out of me."

"Be serious."

"I am. You're different than most of the people I've met in my life."

"Wait a minute, I think you better explain."

"Forget it," he said, already regretting his words.

"There's that toughness again. I guess you need that when you're competing in business."

"But not when you're dancing?"

"I don't know," she said reflectively. "A hard edge, especially in the tango, can lend a certain sparkle to the dance that is hard to describe or even to teach. You just have to have it." She flipped the Off switch on the tape recorder in a sudden decision. "Now that you've gotten the idea of feeling emotion in your dancing, let's go back to the basics. Steps and counts."

"I'm thirsty. Let's take a break, have a drink."

"You just finished your beer."

He stared down at the empty bottle bemusedly. "Maybe some water, then."

"You're stalling."

"I just need some water. Are you sure I can't get you something?"

She shrugged and then threw up her hands. "Fine, we'll take a break."

"So what happened at your school today?" Nicholas asked as they walked down the hallway to the kitchen.

"Water pipe broke," she stated succinctly. "Water, water everywhere and a heck of a mess. We had to shut down the school. I have a contractor coming in tomorrow to take a look."

"Old buildings usually equal big problems. What would you like to drink?" He opened the refrigerator door, exposing a wide selection of soft drinks, mineral waters and fruit juices.

"Wild cherry," she replied, refusing his offer of a glass.

"What does your insurance company think of the damage?"

"I don't know yet. They're going to send someone out tomorrow. I'm ashamed to admit that we don't have much of a policy. We kept putting it off in favor of lower premiums."

"I've done that myself, but it usually doesn't pay off."

"I know." She held the cool bottle against her hot cheeks and sighed. "Just when I thought all our problems were over—something like this happens. It's definitely the last thing I needed right now."

"Your mother must be pretty upset," he commented, watching a spark of guilt flit through her eyes.

"She will be, but I haven't told her yet. She was out today with Howard, and I didn't have the heart to call and interrupt her. She's so happy about the wedding and the new life ahead of her. I didn't want to do anything to spoil it."

"You care a lot about your mother, don't you?"

"Of course I do. She's my mother, and she's a good person with a big heart. Unfortunately it sometimes leads her into big problems."

"As in three marriages? What do you think about that?" he asked bluntly. "Do you approve?"

She considered his question, struck once again by the coldness in his voice when he asked about her mother. "It's not up to me to approve or disapprove. It's her life."

"But I imagine it's also touched on yours. At least one of those marriages occurred when you were a child."

"More than one," she said candidly. "I was nine when she got married for the second time, and presented me with not only one man but two; my younger brother, Michael, was born shortly thereafter. David was okay. He was friendly and he tried to be like a father to me, but it just didn't work. He wasn't really a family man. That marriage ended when I was fifteen. The three of us have been alone since then. That's when my mother bought the school to help support us."

"It must have been tough going through two divorces."

"A little. The first breakup bothered me more than the second. But I don't want you to get the wrong idea about my mother. She did the best she could for all of us." She paused. "And now, as far as the school is concerned, she wants out, and I want in. I suppose if I'm going to run the school, I'll have to learn how to deal with the problems—the business end, not just the dance."

Nicholas took a long sip of his drink as she deftly changed the subject. "Do you think you can do that?"

"I have to. My main concern right now isn't the money," she continued purposefully, "but finding a place to hold the classes while we're doing repairs. I don't suppose you know of any cheap empty halls, do you?"

He smiled at her determined enthusiasm. "Can't say that I do."

"Oh well, something will turn up, unless . . ."

"What?" he asked guardedly.

"A room at your hotel?" Her smile faded at his solemn expression.

"Tango in my hotel? No, I don't think so."

She stared back at him steadily. "We don't just tango. We also teach ballroom dancing, square dancing, ballet, tap and jazz."

"Fine, but this is an exclusive hotel catering to business conventions and elegant gatherings. I don't see how having a dance school in the middle of it would in any way be an asset."

"Fine. Forget I mentioned it. We probably couldn't afford the rent anyway."

He sighed as she set the bottle down on the table with a resounding thud. "I'm sorry if I insulted you. But business is business. You're too soft, Angelia. You've got to get tougher if you want to run your dance school. There's no room for emotion when you're talking dollars and cents."

"And there is no room for business when you're talking dance," she retorted. "Maybe we can learn from each other, unless of course, you're going to continue stalling on your dance lessons."

The challenge slipped from her lips before she could think about the pros and cons of continuing to work with Nicholas Hunter. The man would probably never learn to dance and would only drive her crazy with his unemotional, logical reasoning. But still she was intrigued. There was more to this man than he was showing. And if he was so lacking in feelings, why was he fighting so hard not to learn the tango? Why did it seem to bother him so much? It didn't make sense.

"I'm not stalling," Nicholas said finally. "I'm merely examining a few other options."

"Of course. Well, I'll leave you to it."

"I'm sure you can find something else that's more suitable for your school," he added. "I'll have my secretary make some calls for you tomorrow."

"That won't be necessary. I can handle my own problems. Now, if we're not going to dance, I think I'll be going."

She breezed down the hallway, propelled by frustration and anger and a strange sense of longing. Grabbing her sweater, she headed for the front door, only to be stopped by his hand on her shoulder.

"What?" she demanded.

"Your purse. You left it on the sofa."

She took the purse in her hand, feeling slightly foolish. "Thank you."

His eyes darkened as he sighed. "I'm sorry about the lesson. I guess I wasted another hour of your time."

"I'm afraid so. I don't understand your reluctance to dance, Nicholas. It's a great way to work out tension, to express yourself creatively. I think it might be a nice change for you. But it's your choice."

"Yes, it is. Good night, Angelia."

"Maybe we should just make it goodbye."

He nodded slowly, weighing the wisdom of her words. "Maybe we should."

His ready agreement made her stomach turn over in dismay, and she stared at him in silence, wishing she could take back her impulsive statement, but it was too late.

"Good night," she muttered as he closed the door between them, decisively dividing their worlds.

Chapter Four

Nicholas paced back and forth in his office, waiting for Martin to finish a phone call to their corporate attorney. He hoped the news would be good news, but when Martin finally did hang up the phone his expression was grim.

"The clause is legal," Martin said. "Juan Carlos can set any conditions to the contract that he wants to. Shall I call Angelia?"

"No." He dug his hands into his pockets, racking his brain for another solution. "I'd like to prepare a lengthy report to go along with the plans and the financial information."

"Detailing what?"

"Our feelings for Argentina, the culture, the land, the emotions of the people. You know the routine."

"You think you're going to write your way out of this?" Martin asked skeptically.

"It's a hell of a lot better than dancing."

"You're wasting your time and your money. Juan Carlos doesn't want to read a report put together by your staff. He wants a meeting of the minds with you. Why can't you just dance the tango? It's the simplest solution."

"I can't do it."

"Do you want to explain?"

"No. But I do want that report on my desk by tomorrow afternoon."

Martin got to his feet, shaking his head along the way. "Fine. Spin your wheels, buddy." He picked up the drawing of their proposed resort and spread it out on the desk. "Do you really want to give all this up? Because it's going to come down to this or the dance. I guarantee it."

"We'll see," Nicholas said quietly. "I have a call into Juan Carlos. I'm hoping we can come to a meeting of the minds, as you called it."

"And if you don't?"

"Then I'll do what I have to do."

By three o'clock the next afternoon, Nicholas knew what he had to do; he just didn't know if he could. His conversation with Juan Carlos had been less than satisfactory. In fact the tango seemed to have become the most important issue in the old man's mind. He was putting it ahead of everything including money and logic. Although he had agreed to read a special report, Juan Carlos had said flat out that it wouldn't change his mind. But there was a slim possibility, and that's what he was hanging on to.

Nicholas smiled at his unusual optimism. He didn't lie to himself about anything, but the tango was turning his clear, concise mind upside down. Every time

Angelia put the music on, he started to feel things, and the last thing he wanted to do was feel. He had turned off his emotions twenty-eight years earlier, when his mother had left him. But there was something about Angelia and the damn tango that brought everything back to the surface, the insecurities that had plagued him throughout childhood and the feeling that he wasn't good enough.

He could still remember going to his first high school dance in a pair of secondhand pants that were too short. The kids had laughed and called them floods. And it had gotten worse when he had asked Stephanie Hastings to dance. Stephanie. A beautiful blond cheerleader with a bright smile and legs that went on forever. He had been a fool to think that a girl like that would dance with him. But he had let himself believe for one, long, foolish moment.

He shook his head, forcing the memories back into the locked part of his mind. That time was ancient history. He was successful now, a millionaire, and there were hundreds of Stephanies who would go out with him. And soon he would own the most beautiful strip of land in the world; he would finally reach his ultimate goal. All he had to do was dance—with Angelia.

Angelia. Another part of the problem. He didn't like the way his body reacted to her as if he had no control over his own emotions. But he did have control. He just had to exercise it. She was a dance teacher, and he needed to learn how to dance. It was a logical association. They could dance together, and that would be the end of it. He could make things work.

With that thought in mind, he squared his shoulders and picked up the phone. He would offer her a simple business deal. Everything would be logical, concise, clear-cut, no gray areas, no emotions. Simple.

"You want me to go to Argentina with you?" Angelia asked incredulously, staring at the telephone receiver as if it were a snake.

"Is there a problem?" Nicholas inquired, having already explained his solution to their problem. He would let her use the ballroom of his hotel if she would go to Argentina with him and dance the tango.

"Of course there's a problem," she cried, her mind whirling with the implications of his casual statement. Go back to the land where she was born, see all the places she remembered, dance the tango where it had first originated, see her father...no, she couldn't.

"If you come to Argentina with me, I'll let you use the ballroom at the Plaza for free. It's a good offer, Angelia. You won't find anything better."

"I don't think so," she said abruptly, shaking her head, the movement getting stronger as she thought more about his proposition. "No, I can't go back there."

"I thought you told me that you still missed the country, that a part of you wanted to go back."

"And another part of me doesn't. I have a business to run here. I can't just leave. And there's my mother's wedding."

"She'll be married and on her honeymoon before you have to leave. And I'm sure that one of the other teachers could take over for you. We can cut the trip short, three days, whatever it takes."

"No, I'm sorry."

"This is a perfect solution. You need a place to run your dance classes, and I need a partner."

"But you hate the idea of a dance school in your elegant hotel," she argued.

"It doesn't thrill me. But it's only for a few weeks. I can live with it."

"I just can't drop everything and go to Argentina with you."

"Why not? I thought you were spontaneous, a person who grabs life with both hands."

"I just can't," she whispered. "Don't push it. I'll find someone else for you. Perhaps one of the women in the group tango class would be willing to help you out."

"I don't want any other partner but you."

"It won't work. I can't go back there."

Nicholas bit back a muttered curse. "Don't say no right now. Just think about it for a few days."

"It won't matter."

"Maybe not," he conceded. "But sometimes you don't have a perfect option to choose from. You just have to play the cards the way they were dealt."

"And that's what you're doing—dancing the tango so you can get what you want."

"Yes. Of course, you have to decide just how important your dance school is to you."

Angelia closed her eyes, recognizing the challenge in his voice. "Stop. I get the picture. I'll think about it."

His voice sharpened. "I'll need an answer by tomorrow. If you won't go to Argentina, I'll have to find another partner."

"I can't possibly give you an answer by tomorrow," she complained, annoyed at his high-handed attitude.

"Then the deal's off. It's your choice."

Angelia stared at the phone as he clicked off with a muttered goodbye. She had thought things couldn't possibly get any worse, but now...

Go back to Argentina, the place where everything had started and ended? Could she? Dared she?

The solution Nicholas had come up with was definitely her best offer. She didn't need to look at the long sheet of halls and auditoriums to know that there was nothing that even came close to what he was offering, not in terms of price or space or anything.

If she didn't keep the classes going, she would have to refund money, money that she didn't have. The bank had agreed that a loan might be okayed, but the paperwork would take time, more time than she had.

But the thought of going back to Argentina filled her with illogical terror. She had toyed with the idea in the past, but something had always come up to prevent it. First she had been too young. Then her mother had refused to help her with money or travel arrangements, and finally she had let her commitments build up until there was no possible time to get away. Why?

Because she was afraid of seeing her father again, of feeling the pain that had haunted her dreams every night after their long trip to the United States. All those years without a word from the man who had fathered her, who was supposed to love her, had taken a toll on even her unflagging optimism. But knowing something deep down in her heart was different than coming to face it. If she went to Argentina, there would be no escape.

Or would there? She didn't have to see him. She could just go there, dance the tango and come home. And by doing so, the future of the school would be looking better than it had in a long time. The Pasadena Park Hotel was the perfect answer.

"Come in," she replied absently as a knock at the door cut into her thoughts.

Ricardo stepped over the crowded pile of boxes they were storing away from the water-damaged floors and handed her an estimate sheet. "The contractors said it will take at least four weeks, probably eight to repair the damage to the floors and to redo the plumbing."

Angelia accepted the long proposal gingerly, her mouth curving down into a frown as she read through the legal terms of bids and payment plans. Not much of it made sense, with the minor exception of the figures in black at the bottom of the sheet. Money and time, those were two things she did understand. "I'll show this to my mother," she said wearily. "Thanks for taking them around."

"No problem. I think this group is the best of the bunch."

"I'll pass that on."

"Did you have lunch yet?" Ricardo asked with concern. "You look exhausted."

"I didn't get much sleep last night," she admitted. "I never realized the business end of the school was going to be so time-consuming."

"That's because you're an artist at heart."

"True, but without a studio, we have no place to practice our art."

"Surely one of those halls is available."

"Not on more than a day-by-day program. They have different events scheduled in, and I don't think we can keep moving around and expect the students to follow."

"Are you saying we're going to shut down for the duration?"

She shook her head, seeing the worry in her heart reflected in his eyes. The school was important to them both, but even Ricardo didn't understand how much it meant to her. "No, I'm not saying that at all. In fact, with any luck, we should be able to reopen it by Monday."

"Where?"

"I'll let you know tomorrow. Wish me luck."

"Break a leg."

She smiled and grabbed her purse off the desk. Forty minutes later she was standing in front of a gold placard bearing Nicholas Hunter's name and a very solid oak door. The secretary behind her had already announced her presence, but for just a moment she was completely intimidated. His world was so different from hers. How could she bring her free spirit into this corporate environment?

Her hand hovered above the knob, but before she could move, the door was thrown open and she was face-to-face with Nicholas.

"I thought you needed time to make a decision," he said tensely. "Come in."

"I think fast under pressure," she said, following him into the luxury suite he called an office. "Nice place you have here."

He shrugged his shoulders awkwardly. "It works."

"It certainly does." She paused, running her hand along the top of one leather-backed chair. "I guess you take all this for granted, don't you?"

"Why do you say that?"

"You have a beautiful home, a fantastic office, great clothes ... everything a man could want."

"So?"

She waved her hand toward an antique grandfather clock. "So why don't you act more excited by it all? You have so much, but you don't seem to appreciate it."

"Sit down, Angelia."

She stared at him and then did as she was told.

He picked up a gold-inlaid pen and tossed it idly in the air, catching it before it could hit the top of the mahogany desk. "I do appreciate all this. I just don't like to talk about it."

"Why not?"

"Because it's not important." He waved a hand around the room. "This stuff is window dressing. It makes my guests feel like they're in the most beautiful hotel on earth, and it makes my bankers feel that my success is undoubtable."

"And how does it make you feel?"

"Why don't we talk about why you're here? I must admit I thought it would take a little more than an hour for you to make a decision."

She settled back in her chair, smoothing her floral knit dress down on her thighs. She had thrown the dress on almost as an afterthought. Now she was glad that she had. She felt a little more confident facing him as a businesswoman than a dancer. Although she had to admit that her dress fell far short of the elegance that surrounded Nicholas in his office and his home.

"Well," he prodded, his jaw working a little tensely.

"I've decided to accept your offer."

"Good." He nodded approvingly.

"I hope you'll still think so after we move in."

"So do I."

He smiled back at her so warmly she felt her stomach turn over.

"I didn't think you were planning to go through with the tango, though. I was surprised by your call," she added.

"I wasn't planning to go through with it. In fact I'm still hoping to find a way out, but in the meantime..."

"You'll learn how to dance."

"Yes."

"What happens to me if your trip to Argentina falls through?" she asked bluntly, trying to foresee any more difficulties arising in her life.

"Nothing. I've agreed to let you use my hotel for six weeks. If I cancel the trip to Argentina, you can congratulate yourself for having made such an excellent deal."

"I'll keep that in mind. Now, would it be all right if I went down to the ballroom?"

"Of course. In fact I'm free for the rest of the afternoon, so I'd be happy to show you around."

After relaying a few messages to his secretary, he escorted her down to the mezzanine level where the ballrooms were located. As they walked through the hotel, they were followed by smiles and welcomes, employees preening before the boss, Angelia thought, but Nicholas seemed oblivious to it all. Finally he opened the door to the grand ballroom, and they stepped inside.

The glittering of the chandeliers took her breath away, and for a moment she just stood and stared. It was a gorgeous room even in its starkness. The hardwood floors would be perfect for their dance classes, and in this atmosphere perhaps even the most stumbling ballroom dancers would be able to find their rhythm, matching the elegance of their steps to the elegance of the room. It was the perfect setting.

"What do you think?" he asked.

She tossed her head and grinned. "It works."

He smiled back at her. "Good. Do we have a deal?"

"Yes. Yes. Yes." She took a few impulsive steps, whirling around the room, her full skirt whipping around her legs. "This is a wonderful room. I can't wait to bring my students in here. In fact we may never leave."

"Six weeks," he said matter-of-factly. "After that we renegotiate."

"I can live with that." She smiled joyously, feeling the burdens of the past twenty-four hours floating off her shoulders. "You don't know how much this is going to help me. I feel like celebrating, kicking up my heels." She did a brief jitterbug step in front of his amazed eyes. "Dance with me, Nick."

"No way. I'm not dancing with you here."

The look of discomfort on his face made her laugh. "Chicken. This is a great place."

"Anyone could come in. What would they think if they saw the boss tangoing in the ballroom with no music? They'd think I was crazy."

"Or maybe just human." She dropped her hand. "But I do feel like celebrating, and since you and I are going to be partners, I think it's time we got better acquainted."

He sent her a wary look. "What did you have in mind?"

She hesitated for a split second, but the tempting blue in his eyes made her throw caution to the wind. She really did want to get to know him better. "Dinner. It's almost five, and I'm hungry. Unless you have plans?"

"I was going to have a drink with one of my managers, but I suppose I could postpone it," he said slowly. "Where would you like to eat? We have a very nice restaurant here, two actually, one formal, one casual. I can almost guarantee a perfect meal."

She thought about his suggestion but found it strangely unappealing. Here in the hotel he would still be Nicholas Hunter, boss, reserved, formal and probably not a lot of fun. She wanted to dig deeper, find out what he was really like away from all the signs of his success. "It sounds nice, but I'd like to get away, and I'm sure you could use a break from this place."

"I'm very comfortable here. But it's up to you, of course. I'll just go upstairs and let my secretary know we're leaving."

"Fine. I'll meet you in the lobby." She walked to the door with him, parting company as they came to the escalator. Taking a seat in one of the lounge chairs, she took several deep breaths and tried to relax. She had solved the dance school dilemma, but now she had something else to worry about—Argentina and the very sexy Nicholas Hunter.

"Where are we going?" Nicholas asked as he helped her into the front seat of a sleek blue Mercedes. "Do you want to stop at your apartment to change clothes?''

"Do I look that bad?" she questioned lightly.

"No," he said hastily. "But if you want to go fancy, you might feel more comfortable in something more formal.''

"I don't think we need to bother. Nothing in my closet would match up to the way you look," she said slightly ruefully but with pride in her eyes. "I'm afraid we live in two very different worlds.''

"Just because a person has Shakespeare on the shelves of his library doesn't mean that he actually reads it," Nicholas replied, gunning the engine.

She looked at him in surprise. "So you're saying you're a fake?''

"I would never say that." He tossed her a casual smile, one of the few she had seen from him. "So, what's it going to be? French, Italian, Continental?''

"I do have an idea, but it's a bit of a drive. Are you up to it?''

"Why does every word that comes out of your mouth sound like a challenge?''

She sent him a sublime smile. "I can't imagine.''

"Right. Let's go." He pushed the button above their heads, opening the sunroof and letting the late-afternoon sunshine flow through the car.

"Just get on the freeway and head toward the Santa Monica Beach.''

"A nice restaurant overlooking the beach, huh?''

"You'll find out soon enough." She laughed as the scowl returned to his face, but when he turned to look at her, there was a lurking smile in his eyes. "Just drive. I'll let you know where to go.''

Chapter Five

Angelia laughed breathlessly as Nicholas turned off the freeway and drove down the highway along the Santa Monica Beach. Her dark hair was blowing around her face from the windy drive, and her cheeks were flushed as she turned to look at him.

"You drive like a maniac. Do you know that?"

He grinned at the look of bemusement on her face. "Sorry, it's one of my vices. I like to go fast."

"No kidding. I don't think your foot even touched the brake. You've completely destroyed your image of conservative, cautious businessman."

"Never. I drive fast but not recklessly, and I own a car that is maintained in excellent condition. The tires are new, the fluids are cleaned regularly and the brakes are constantly checked for wear. I've driven thousands of miles in all conditions and I've even taken some lessons in speed racing. There's really nothing left to chance."

She waved a hand to stop his mini lecture. "Stop. I take it back. You have no passion in your soul, only logic and perhaps a little thirst for speed."

He grinned. "I know it sounds boring, but I like to know exactly what I'm working with."

"I get the picture."

"So where is this restaurant we're going to?" He looked out the window, searching for a sign. On one side of the road was the sparkling blue of the Pacific Ocean and on the other, jagged cliffs separating the rest of the city from the beach. It was a clear and fairly warm day for February but still too early in the season to draw more than a few locals strolling along the sand.

Angelia smiled as she directed him into a nearly empty beach parking lot at the bottom of the pier. "Right over there."

"I don't see anything but a hamburger stand."

"That's Rico's. He makes the best chili burgers in town. They're hot and spicy and incredibly good. You'll love it."

"You're kidding, right?"

"Don't you like hamburgers?"

With a shake of his head he followed her out of the car and over to the one-man stand.

"Hi, Rico, I brought you a new customer."

"He's okay," was the aging Rico's reply as his weather-beaten eyes glanced appraisingly down Nicholas's fine suit. "A little overdressed, but I'll give you lots of napkins."

"Thanks."

"We're really going to eat hamburgers?" Nicholas asked with a puzzled look in his eyes.

"Chili burgers," she corrected. "They'll raise your cholesterol a hundred points, but they're definitely worth it. I'll have a chili burger with the works, an order of fries and a vanilla milk shake," she added. "What about you?"

Nicholas shrugged, taking off his designer sunglasses. "I'll have the same."

"You don't really mind, do you?" she asked hesitantly. "We can go somewhere else if you like."

"Just tell me one thing, did we really spend an hour on the freeway to get to a hamburger stand?"

"I know it seems crazy, but I love Rico's burgers and the beach and this seemed like a good place to get away. Neutral territory, so to speak."

"Maybe you're right. It's been a long time since I've had a casual dinner, no fancy wines or arrogant waiters. I can live with this." He looked into her twinkling brown eyes and thought he could probably live with just about anything as long as she kept smiling at him.

"Good. I think you'll enjoy it."

He shrugged off his suit coat while they were waiting, loosened his tie and rolled up the sleeves on his white shirt without giving her a second glance, but she couldn't help watching this intriguing revelation. He seemed to be not only shedding his outer clothes but also the air of aloofness that he wore so well. In fact, in the late-afternoon sunshine, he looked much younger and more relaxed, almost like a young man on holiday instead of a businessman grabbing an early dinner.

"We can eat over there," she said, as they picked up their order.

Over there was a pile of large boulders that looked out at the crashing waves. Nicholas nodded and followed her across the sand, climbing over the boulders until they found two that were reasonably flat and wide enough to accommodate their bodies and their burgers.

"This looks great," Angelia proclaimed, picking up the dripping cheeseburger with a smile that bordered on greedy. "I'm starved."

Nicholas smiled and took a bite. Five minutes later he stared at her empty wrapper and then back at his half-eaten hamburger in bemusement. "Where did it go?"

"I told you I was hungry."

"You eat faster than I do, and I've been known to set a few records in my time."

"I know. It's a terrible habit. My mother always says, slow down, Angelia. It's not ladylike to gulp. It's not proper to finish your food before everyone else at the table." She laughed and pulled her legs up under her body, getting into a more comfortable position.

Once again they were silent, preferring to listen to the sounds of the beach, the cries of the sea gulls, the distant laughter of children throwing rocks into the waves and the final, reassuring crash of water against sand, marking the time with its own peculiar sense of rhythm.

The sun began to settle on the distant horizon, shades of pink and orange eclipsing the blue of the sky. Angelia had seen a lot of sunsets in her time, but there was something about this sunset, this moment, that was different than anything she had ever experienced.

Nicholas. She knew he was the reason for the ridiculous feeling of pleasure that was creeping along her spine. She just wasn't sure what she should do about it. She knew next to nothing about him except that he liked business, hated to dance, was far too logical. He was also sexy and appealing. Too appealing.

"This is nice," she muttered, searching for sane, methodical words that would break up the feeling of longing that was hitting her as hard as the waves against the beach.

"I've always liked the ocean," he agreed. "It keeps coming in, no matter how far it gets dragged back. It's just relentless, working away at the sand, piece by piece."

She sent him a curious look, but his eyes were fixed on the water and his expression was still carefully guarded.

"I like it, too. It reminds me of Argentina. The town I was born in is very near the water. We lived there part of the year and the rest of the year in Buenos Aires, where my father worked. I never felt as comfortable in the city as I did down by the water."

"Or as you do in the dance studio."

"I think that's the place I feel the most comfortable. What about you?"

"Me?" He shrugged his shoulders, thinking, weighing his words. "I've learned how to fit in."

She nodded slowly. "Yes, you remind me of a pet I once had."

His blue eyes widened involuntarily as he turned to face her. "A pet?"

"That got your attention."

"What kind of a pet? Or should I ask?"

"A lizard."

"A lizard? Great. I'm glad I'm making such a good impression."

She laughed lightly. "A chameleon actually, the kind of lizard that changes color to fit into the environment so that it can slink away whenever it wants. That's why you're learning the tango, isn't it? So that you can fit into the Argentine environment."

"I suppose that's true in a way. But is that bad?"

"I don't know. When we left Argentina, I had a difficult time fitting in with the kids at my new American school. I spoke some English, but with a definite accent. I was a square peg trying to fit into a round hole. I tried very hard to be one of the gang, but I finally realized it was never going to work. So I just stopped trying."

"And now you're free, independent, Angelia. I think you're very lucky."

"Why? Because I'm not trying to fit in anymore?"

"Because you don't feel you have to."

"You're not just talking about the tango, are you, Nick?"

"Do you want to take a walk along the water?" he asked abruptly, sliding off the rocks purposefully.

"As long as we can keep talking."

"About what?"

"You, of course. Why don't you tell me about yourself? I'm a good listener."

"I'm sure you are," he said quietly. "I'm just not much of a talker. I grew up alone. I guess I've gotten used to keeping things to myself."

"What happened to your family?"

"I never had a family. I grew up in an orphanage, spent some time in foster homes, but I never had anyone that really lasted. When I hit eighteen I just went out on my own, and I never looked back.''

"Never?" she asked gently.

"Maybe once in a while," he conceded. "But I realized a long time ago that I might not have had any control over the past, but I sure as hell have control over my future. That's why I plan things out. I like to know where everything is going."

"You've done pretty well for yourself, considering your background. Did you go to college?"

"Two years at the community college and then two years at UCLA. I barely got through on a scholarship and a student loan, but it was worth it."

"And after college you became a millionaire overnight?" she asked teasingly.

He smiled, but it didn't quite reach his eyes. "Hardly overnight. I spent eight years working for a land development company, learning how to build everything from shopping centers to condominiums. Then with a little help from some investors, I managed to open my own company, and the rest is history."

"You make it sound easy, but I'm sure it wasn't." She hugged her arms around her waist as an afternoon breeze ruffled her hair.

"I paid my dues. But everyone has to do that. I've come a long way, but I'm not done yet."

"What else is there to do? What's left?" she asked, her brown eyes sparking with curiosity.

"Argentina, for one."

"Why is that particular strip of land so important to you?"

Nicholas thought of the magazine paper folded carefully away in his desk drawer. Years of yellowing had diminished its beautiful array of colors, but the passing years had heightened the image in his own mind. He still had a childhood fantasy to fulfill. But how could he tell her that?

"Come on, walk with me."

"Sure, why not?" she replied, accepting his change in conversation, at least for the moment. She slipped off her canvas sandals so she could enjoy the sand drifting through her toes, the change from dry to moist as they got nearer to the water.

Nick paused as she walked closer to the incoming tide, and impulsively she let the water drift over her feet and up to her ankles, enjoying the cold sensation against her legs.

"You're crazy," he said from behind her, standing carefully at the edge of the waterline, his leather shoes safely out of reach.

"Why don't you join me?" she cried, laughing as the wind picked up, blowing her skirt higher around her legs.

He looked at her slender figure, silhouetted by the setting sun, and swallowed deeply. She was a picture of life, a beautiful woman, laughing, feeling. The ache in his gut intensified.

"Come on in, it feels wonderful." She extended her hand invitingly.

If only he dared to join her, but he had a feeling that taking her hand and walking into the water would be the biggest step he had ever taken in his life. They were opposites in every way. She didn't want to fit in; he had spent his whole life trying to be accepted.

If he didn't stay focused, if he allowed himself to stray, he might lose everything he had gained, and then he would have to start over again, just like the water, pounding away relentlessly, tirelessly. But he was tired, weary of the role-playing and the games. He wanted to be free. He wanted her.

She laughed as a larger wave rolled in, splashing the edge of her skirt with water. "Whoops. That was a little close."

"You're going to get wet," he warned as another wave came crashing down, spraying her with drops of water. Instinctively he reached out a hand to pull her away from the incoming wave, but as her soft body came into contact with his chest, everything else faded in comparison. She turned naturally into his arms, locking her hands around his waist, staring into his eyes with a desire that matched the rapid beat of his heart. Her lips parted invitingly. He couldn't resist.

He lowered his head and kissed her. The light touch was everything he had dreamed of. Her lips were incredibly soft, supple, and parted easily under the demands of his own mouth. His grip around her tightened as he kissed her again and again, losing himself in the warmth of her mouth. Nothing else mattered, not the wind or the sun or the possibility of onlookers, not even the feeling of water running through his shoes.

Water! He lifted his head in bemusement and stared down at his fine leather shoes, now buried under several inches of water and a pile of seaweed.

Angelia looked at him in confusion, still breathless from his kiss. But as she followed his gaze, she found herself smiling and then laughing. Nicholas tried to frown as he picked one foot up and then the other, but as another wave hit the beach, sending a fresh spray of white foam around his ankles, he started to smile and then laughed out loud.

"This is your fault, you know," he said, trying to infuse a note of seriousness back into his voice as he walked out of the water, picking up sand as he went. He stopped, looked down at his muddy shoes and then back into Angelia's face. She was quiet now, weighing his reaction. "Well, what are you going to do about it?"

She tipped her head back and forth thoughtfully. "I can't afford to buy you new shoes, so I guess I'll just have to try to help you forget about it."

"How are you going to do that?"

"You could kiss me again."

"I didn't kiss you. You kissed me."

"No way. I couldn't reach your lips unless you bent your head."

"You pulled my head down."

"I did not. I just looked at you and all of a sudden—" her eyes sparkled mischievously as she paused "—you were kissing me. Maybe we should reenact the scene of the crime so that we can be sure what happened."

"You're crazy and dangerous," he added, taking a step back. "You've already ruined one pair of my shoes. I don't want to risk anything else."

"You wouldn't," she said perceptively. "And that surprises me. Because I would think risk-taking and business success would go hand in hand."

"They do."

"So you take risks in your business, but not in your personal life."

He stepped out of his shoes, ignoring her question and the speculative gleam in her eyes. "Let's take a walk along the beach. That's what we started out to do. Or do you want to get back?"

"Let's walk." They strolled down to the far end of the beach, each lost in thought, and paused as the sun finally dipped beyond the horizon. "I guess we should leave," she said reluctantly as dusk settled over the beach. "It will be dark in a few minutes."

"All right."

She started to walk and then paused as his hand came down on her shoulder.

"About what happened," he said.

"I'm sorry about your shoes."

He shook his head, his eyes turning a darker, midnight blue. "I'm not talking about my shoes. And I'm the one who should apologize."

"Please don't, Nick. I wanted you to kiss me, or maybe I wanted to kiss you," she said with a touch of their earlier humor. "It felt good."

He smiled but his eyes were still serious. "But I don't want you to think that—"

"That you're interested in me? What are you worried about?"

"I'm a loner, Angelia. I just want you to understand that."

"I didn't ask you for anything. It was just a kiss. Let's go home." She let out a long breath as he strode ahead of her toward the car. Just a kiss, but what a kiss. She felt as if her whole world was turning upside down, and she had a strange feeling that Nick felt the same way.

She waited beside the car as he shrugged his arms back into his suit coat and pulled his tie out of his pocket. If it hadn't been for the bare feet, he would have made a complete transformation to reserved businessman. She watched him with a growing sense of disappointment. He was changing again, and she couldn't do anything to stop it. "What about your dance lessons? Do you want to get together tonight?"

"I'll have to pass. I have work to do."

"All right. I might as well go spread the good news to the rest of the staff. When do you think we can start using the ballroom?"

"Monday, if you like. There's also a spare office along that floor you can set up shop in for the time being."

"That's very considerate of you."

"We have a deal, remember?"

"How could I forget?" she said lightly, a heaviness weighing on her heart as they settled into the car and began the drive back to Pasadena. Their business arrangement was not going to get personal, not if Nicholas Hunter had anything to say about it. But a glance at the taut line of his jaw and the restless jerks of his hands on the steering wheel gave her hope. They were very different people, that was true, but she had always relied on her instincts and deep down she was convinced that the real Nicholas Hunter was going to turn out to be a kindred spirit.

"You always land on your feet, don't you?" Michelle asked with a small smile as she and Angelia walked around the grand ballroom the following Monday. They had spent the weekend moving their records and office essentials, and the last thing on their list was the placement of room dividers.

"We have a business deal," Angelia replied. "There is nothing else going on."

"Of course not. So tell me what exactly are the terms of your business deal?"

"It doesn't really concern you."

"I do still own the school. I think I have a right to know what arrangements you've made."

Angelia sighed, staring back at her mother with a troubled gaze. There was no point in evading the inevitable. She would find out sooner or later. "I'm going to Argentina with him to dance the tango."

Her mother's slender hand flew to her mouth, horror dawning in her beautiful green eyes. "No, you're not going back there."

"It's only for a couple of days. Nicholas has to perform the tango in order to complete a business transaction for some land that he wants to buy. It's just one dance."

"No, I won't allow you to go."

"I don't think you really have that option," Angelia reminded her gently.

"Then I'll go with you."

"That won't work, either. We're not going until the week after your wedding. You'll be on your honeymoon by then."

"I'll just have to postpone the wedding," Michelle said tightly. "We'll have to get married later. Unless there's any way I can talk you out of this?"

Angelia shook her head, her own doubts resurfacing in the face of her mother's worry. Why didn't she want her to go back to Argentina? What could she possibly learn after eighteen years of silence?

"Why do you have to do this?" Michelle asked desperately. "Why now, when everything is coming together for us?"

"It wasn't my first choice, believe me. But we needed a place to hold our classes, and this was the perfect solution. I don't want to hear any more arguments or talk about canceling your wedding. You've been waiting a long time for the right man, and if you think Howard Bellerman is it, then I don't want you to wait any longer. I'm a big girl now, and in case you're wondering, I'm not planning on seeing him anyway."

"You're not? Why not? I mean, you always seem so anxious to hear about the past." Michelle tripped over her words in agitation.

"Maybe I'm a little bit of a coward. Or maybe I just don't want to dredge up all those old memories."

"You won't be able to avoid them if you go to Argentina."

"Perhaps not. But I am going. The past is the past, but my future is the school, and I'm not going to do anything to jeopardize that. Our classes will start in here tomorrow."

Michelle sighed. "I can see I'm not going to be able to change your mind. Just promise me that you won't try to contact him."

Angelia shook her head. "I can't promise you that. I'm not planning on it, but I just can't promise." She hesitated for a long moment. "I wish you could just tell me what happened."

"We didn't get along. Leave it at that."

"How can I? Don't you realize that it affects me even now? That I find it difficult to get involved with anyone because I don't understand what happened? I thought you two had a happy, loving marriage. Then one day you wake me up, and we leave Argentina in the middle of the night. How can I trust my instincts when I was so wrong about you both?"

"You were a child. You couldn't have known what was going on."

"But I'm an adult now, and I think you should tell me the truth."

"I don't know what the truth is anymore." Michelle shook her head, her eyes misting over with tears. "I've tried to forget everything about those years in Argentina. And you should do the same. Forget this trip, forget everything. Just start from now and don't let my mistakes hurt you. We're not the same, Angelia. You're much stronger and smarter. When you choose a man, it will be the right man. I'm sure of it."

Angelia sighed. It was always the same. She asked questions and her mother parried each one like a well-trained boxer. If she wanted answers, she was going to have to find them somewhere else. "Thanks for your vote of confidence," she said.

Michelle held out her arms in a gesture of affection, and Angelia slipped into her embrace, giving her a tight, fierce hug. It was a turning point for both of them, recognition of their changing relationship. Michelle was the first to draw back, blinking away the moisture in her eyes. "So, tell me about Nicholas Hunter. Are you two seeing each other?"

Angelia laughed out loud. "You never quit, do you? Come on, I'll treat you to lunch in the café downstairs. The dessert tray has been haunting me since I walked by early this morning."

They were lingering over coffee and discussing wedding plans when Nicholas walked into the café with two other men. She saw him before he saw her, but still she wasn't prepared for the desire that flared in his eyes as he looked up and caught her staring. For just a moment the look was totally unguarded, revealing a depth of emotion that was so often absent in their conversations.

When the hostess stepped between them, she let out a long, ragged breath.

"Is something wrong?" Michelle questioned, discreetly turning her chair so she could see what was attracting Angelia's gaze. Her lips curved in a knowing smile as Nicholas and the two other men walked toward their table.

"Hello, Mr. Hunter," Michelle said brightly as he paused to greet them. He motioned to his associates to take a seat at one of the tables a few feet away.

"Hello," he said, bestowing a brief courteous smile on her mother that deepened as he turned to face her. "How are the plans coming along for the ballroom?"

"Fine, we should be able to start classes tomorrow."

"That's good."

She nodded, unable to look away from his piercing blue eyes. She wished her mother, his business associates and the rest of the restaurant would disappear for a moment, so that she could just look at him, talk to him, touch the tiny dimple along his jawline that made his face look utterly appealing.

"I hope you'll come to my wedding, Mr. Hunter," Michelle interjected when they were both silent.

"That's very thoughtful of you," Nicholas said, clearing his throat. "It's on Saturday, isn't it?"

"Yes. Valentine's Day. We'd really love to have you, unless of course you have a valentine to take care of."

"Not at the moment," he replied dryly.

"You can think about it," Angelia put in, not wanting Nicholas to be caught up in her mother's manipulations but secretly hoping he would accept.

"I'd like to come," he said.

"Good. I'll make sure you get an invitation."

"Thank you. I'm afraid I'll have to excuse myself now. I have a lunch meeting. I hope the ballroom and the office space are adequate. If you need anything at all, please don't hesitate to call me."

"I will," Angelia said politely, wishing that they could put the social greetings aside and really talk. She was beginning to want much more from him than polite conversation, and the intensity of her emotions was startling. Despite her free-spirit nature, deep down she had always been wary of men and intimate relationships, but Nicholas was pushing all of her careful caution to the wayside, and he wasn't even trying.

That was the real joke. Nicholas Hunter might be attracted, but it was very obvious that he had no intention of doing anything about it. He didn't want to get involved with her. He just wanted a tango partner, someone to make him look good for his associates. She had to stop thinking there was going to be anything more between them. With a sigh she tossed her napkin onto her plate.

"Are you ready to go?" Michelle asked, fixing her lipstick.

"Yes," Angelia said firmly, getting to her feet. "I need some air." At the very least, she added under her breath as they walked out of the restaurant.

After exchanging goodbyes, she spent the rest of the day on the phone calling up students and reinitiating classes. By seven o'clock that evening, her makeshift office was organized and the classes were completely rescheduled to begin the next day. She had nothing left to do except stop by the bridal salon on her way home and try on her dress.

Stop dawdling, she told herself, taking another look at the clock. Nicholas was not going to return her phone calls. She had tried to contact him several times during the day to confirm their next tango lesson, but his secretary had consistently told her he was in a meeting and would get back to her. She had no idea if that was the standard excuse or the truth, but perhaps it was just as well he wasn't available. She needed some space, some time to put her feelings about him into perspective.

The knock at her door sent a tingle down her spine, and instinctively she knew who it was. "Come in."

Chapter Six

"I understand you've been looking for me," Nicholas said, stepping into her office.

"Yes, I was wondering about our next tango lesson."

"Oh, that."

"We are still going to Argentina next week, aren't we?"

"I definitely am. I'm still not certain about you."

"Has something changed?"

He shook his head, and his mouth curved into a dry smile. "Not yet, but I'm still working on it. After all, there have to be other things besides the tango that someone like Juan Carlos would appreciate." He slid down into the chair in front of her desk. "I've been giving it some thought, and I think I have a new angle."

"What's that?"

"Food."

She smiled at the mischief in his eyes. "You have my attention, go on."

"Maybe I can cook something for him that is strictly Argentine fare, show him that I understand the flavor of his country."

"Very good," she said, clapping her hands together in mock applause. "But I think if you spent as much time learning the tango as you do trying to get out of it, you'd be an expert by now. Level with me, Nick. Why don't you want to dance with me?"

He stared back at her, his smile downgrading into a frown. "It's not you. I hate to dance. And the last thing I want to do is make a fool of myself."

"You won't. Not if we practice."

"I'm not so sure about that."

"Can you cook better than you can dance?"

He tipped his head thoughtfully. "No, but I think cooking something would be a hell of a lot easier to handle than doing the tango for him and his wide circle of friends."

"I don't know about that. You might poison somebody."

"I'm not that bad. Anyone can read directions."

She grinned at his smug tone. "Why don't we see if that's true. Since it doesn't look like I'm going to get you to dance. Why don't you cook me dinner tonight?"

"Tonight? I don't have any food or recipes," he added hastily.

"I do. In fact I'll even help you out. I'll make you a shopping list of everything you need to buy at the store. Then you can bring it over to my place and cook it according to my recipe. What could be easier?"

He stared at her in dismay. "This is a trick, right?"

"Any simpleton can make a meal," she reminded him, her amusement flowing at his expense. "It's dinner or the tango. Take your pick."

"Fine. Write it down," he ordered abruptly. "And give me directions to your place. I'm going to cook you a meal you'll never forget."

Angelia had no idea how dinner was going to turn out, but she knew she would never forget the sight of Nicholas sweating it out over a bowl and a cookbook. His initial arrogance had quickly faded as he tried to interpret the special language universal to cooks but completely foreign to everyone else.

She laughingly refused to help him with the directions even when her stomach began to growl hungrily, although she did take dessert and drinks out of his hands, whipping up a traditional flan and heating up some maté, a favorite tea in Argentina.

"The empanadas or whatever you call them are ready," Nicholas said finally, pulling his meat pie out of the oven with trepidation. "I hope you're not too hungry."

She peered over his shoulder at the thickening mass that was burnt on one side and still uncooked in the middle. "What on earth is that? It doesn't look like the picture."

"I did exactly what the recipe said. I don't know what happened. I don't think the flour was supposed to thicken like it did. Maybe it was bad. I couldn't find a date on it anywhere," he said accusingly. "In fact your kitchen is an accident waiting to happen. I found some cheese in there that was completely green."

"Cleaning out my refrigerator has never been high on my list. How much flour did you use?" she asked, ignoring his complaints.

"Three tablespoons, like it said."

Angelia reached over to the recipe book lying on the counter. "Three teaspoons, Nick. That's the smaller spoon."

"I know that. Damn. I must have just misread it. In fact it looks like there is a line through part of it."

She stared down at the cookbook, licked her finger and then pressed it to the line he was talking about. Then she lifted it up to show him. "It's your eyelash. Make a wish."

"A wish?" he asked in confusion. "What the hell are you talking about now? Is wishing going to make this dinner palatable?"

She laughed. "Only if your wish is answered. Come on, make a wish and then blow the lash away."

"That's silly."

"So what. It might come true. Go on, live a little," she encouraged.

He shook his head in resignation, finally lowering his head and then blowing the lash off her finger.

"What did you wish for?" she asked with irrepressible curiosity.

"I don't think I'm supposed to say."

"How would you know? You didn't even know about the tradition. Didn't anyone ever tell you about it?" Her voice trailed away as a sudden flash of pain darkened his blue eyes. "They didn't, did they?"

"I learned early on that wishes don't come true. You have to make things happen in your life. Nothing just comes to you, no matter how badly you want it."

"That's true," she said quietly. "I used to wish that my father would come and see us. But he never did."

"So you stopped wishing."

She shook her head. "Maybe for that, but not for other things. I just can't seem to stop. I think that good things do happen, sometimes unexpectedly. And what's the harm in hoping?"

"Hoping usually ends in disappointment. It's better to set reasonable goals and then work toward them."

"I agree. But there's always that one intangible that makes some goals become reality and others not. It's called luck."

Nicholas smiled at the bright expression in her eyes. "And I suppose you still believe in Santa Claus, too."

"You never know," she said airily. "The impossible can happen."

"The odds are against it."

"I don't like to play the odds. In fact I like the long shots the best. If you win, you win big."

"But the risk is greater."

"So is the fun. Take this meal, for instance. I knew it was definitely a long shot that you would be able to cook, but I was willing to take the risk," she teased.

"And you lost," he retorted. "That's what happens when you go with the long shot. I still don't know why it burned on the outside."

"You were supposed to cover it while it was cooking and then uncover it for the last ten minutes just to brown the top."

"It didn't say that."

"You have to read the fine print. Didn't they teach you that in business school? Don't look so grim. At least we've had fun."

"Speak for yourself," he grumbled, stifling a smile as she reached for his pie.

She turned on the light over the stove so she could examine it more closely, but there was nothing salvageable about it. She stuck a knife into the middle, and it stood upright without her touching it. When she tried to pull it out, it wouldn't budge. She stared at it incredulously and then started to giggle, finally turning it into a full-blown laugh.

"Stop it," Nicholas said half-heartedly, his own lips curving into a reluctant smile. "It's not that bad."

"It looks worse than the mud pies I used to make as a kid." She laughed again, her sense of fun so contagious that Nicholas eventually joined in. And then her laughter died. Because the sight of Nicholas smiling and laughing was one she had never seen before, and it touched her deeply. He was a mess with flour down his light blue shirt and spatters of grease on his tie and chin. There was even a smudge of paprika over one eyebrow. Without thought she reached up her hand to wipe it off, and then his laughter died, too.

He caught her hand at the wrist, his blue eyes darkening as he allowed her fingers to trail down the side of his face. Then suddenly his hands were cupping her own face, tilting it up so that her lips were just inches from his mouth. And then he bent his head and kissed her, his tongue gently pushing past her teeth into the warm cavern of her mouth. It was a hungry kiss filled with wanting and longing.

She wrapped her arms around his neck, holding him close, kissing him back when she thought he was stopping, letting her fingers roam through the curls at the base of his neck, pulling him closer until the hard edge of his chest was pushing against the softness of her breasts.

Finally, breathlessly, he pulled away, reaching up a hand to wipe a smudge of flour by the corner of her mouth, the intimate gesture becoming more personal as her tongue slipped out to lick the flour off his finger.

He sucked in his breath at the motion, his eyes catching with hers in unmistakable desire. "Lord, Angelia, you almost make me believe in the impossible." He took a deliberate step back. "I think whatever is on my face is now on yours. Sorry about that."

She eyed the distance between them with a frown. "Don't be sorry. I liked it."

Her brown eyes were once again challenging, and he couldn't help smiling. "You definitely taste better than my pie."

"I don't think that would be too hard." She paused, her brown eyes turning solemn. "Nick . . ."

He put a finger over her lips. "Don't ask."

"You don't know what I was going to say."

"Knowing your penchant for unpredictability, that's probably true," he said with a light smile that was at odds with the serious expression in his eyes. "Just leave it alone for now."

After a long, tense moment, she nodded. "For now."

He turned and sighed. "I think we can get rid of this." He turned the pie over, dumping the contents into the sink. Then he scraped the pan and turned the water and the garbage disposal on, successfully destroying the intimacy that had grown between them.

He didn't want to talk about what had happened. He didn't want to admit that there was something growing between them, that the thought of kissing her senseless and slowly unbuttoning the knit top that clung to her breasts had even occurred to him. But it had, and definitely more than once. Logically he knew it was a mistake. "Maybe we should order a pizza," he suggested as he turned off the water. "Or go out."

"We don't have to do that. I can make something here for us."

"It's almost eight. You must be starving."

"I am hungry, but I had a feeling this was going to happen, so I defrosted some lasagna I made a few days ago. It's in the microwave."

"You little cheat. You were planning to eat that all along."

"No. I just thought we should have a backup plan."

"A backup plan? You?"

"Sometimes I do think ahead." She walked over to the microwave and pulled out a steaming pan of lasagna she had surreptitiously heated while Nick was working on his meat pie. "It's not typical Argentine fare, but I think you'll like it."

"Actually I'm beginning to wish I'd never even heard of Argentina," he replied, taking a seat at the cozy table in one corner of the kitchen, the only reference to a dining room that she had.

"You don't mean that." She dished out two plates and placed one in front of Nicholas and then sat down to eat. "Wine?"

"Please." He settled back in his chair. "It's true. I've made deals before, but this one is definitely the worst. I'm a businessman, Angelia. I pride myself on logic and rules and appropriate ways to play the game. Juan Carlos is throwing all that out, and it's driving me crazy."

"Sometimes when you throw out the rules, it makes the game more interesting," she suggested.

"Not for me. I've spent years studying my business. I don't like surprises."

"Surprises are the spice of life. They add zing and excitement."

"And sometimes disaster."

"You're not really this cynical, are you?"

"Most of the time. I don't have any reason to be optimistic. The world is basically a dark place."

"And this glass is half empty, right?" She pointed to her wineglass.

"It is," he said agreeably. "I know what you're going to say, but that's just the way I look at things."

"You can change if you want to."

"I don't want to."

She sighed, shaking her head as she considered his statement. The problem was that she didn't think in logical terms; she thought in emotions, feelings, gut instincts. She didn't know how to argue convincingly against someone like Nick. Somehow she would just have to show him that life could be better with a little excitement in it, maybe even a little tango, maybe even her.

"Thanks for saving my stomach," Nick said a few minutes later, finishing his meal. "I owe you one."

"The lasagna was a nice surprise, wasn't it?" she said blandly.

He shook his head at her knowing smirk and began to clean off the table. "Where shall I put these?"

"The sink is fine. I have to unload the dishwasher before we can put those in."

"Let me help you."

"You don't have to do that. I'm sure you don't get much practice loading dishwashers."

"Actually that's one thing I have had a lot of practice in. I worked as a busboy for quite a few years."

"Really? Was that when you were in school?"

"Yeah." He set the dishes down with a clatter, as if regretting his momentary confidence. "I think I'll go wash my hands."

"The bathroom's in there," she said, pointing to the bedroom. Retreat was something Nicholas Hunter had perfected to a science. She just wished she had a better idea exactly what he was running from.

"I think I'll get going," he said, coming back into the kitchen a few minutes later.

She dried her hands on the tea towel and followed him to the front door. "So, where do we stand on the tango?"

"Until I can think of something better, it's back on." He smiled. "But next time I won't involve you."

"I didn't really mind. It was fun. I'm still trying to figure out who you really are."

"There's no mystery. I'm just an ordinary man."

"Not by a long shot. But don't worry, I'm not going to ask any more questions. I hope when you're ready, you'll tell me what I need to know."

His smile disappeared at the seriousness in her voice. "This isn't personal, Angelia. I just don't like to get too close to people."

"I believe you. But I'm not just any person. We're going to have to dance together, Nick. We're going to have to be able to trust each other enough to do that."

"Right." He put his hand on the doorknob and paused. "I'll see you tomorrow."

* * *

But he didn't see her the next day. In fact he seemed to have vanished completely. His secretary said he was in meetings during the day, so she waited until evening and then called his home number, but the only answer was his cryptic male voice reciting his number and requesting a message.

Deciding the next move was his, she concentrated on getting her classes restarted. Tuesday was filled with the normal chaos and confusion, but by Wednesday afternoon things were beginning to run smoothly. The students were enjoying their new surroundings, and the hotel staff had been more than helpful. She was just finishing up a waltz lesson when her mother found her ushering the last of her students out of the ballroom.

"There you are," Michelle said with a weary sigh, following her down the hallway to her office. "I picked up your dress for the wedding, and some special shoes I think would go nicely. And I found the most beautiful crystal wedding tier for the top of the cake. I'd love to take you by the bakery and show it to you. Are you free now?"

Angelia shook her head apologetically. "Unfortunately not. I have another class at four."

"You can't get away?"

"I'm sorry, but things are so new around here, I don't want to do any more switching than I absolutely have to."

"I suppose you're right," Michelle said with disappointment. "But I wish you had a little more time to be involved with the wedding. It's only three days away."

"I know. Maybe tonight we can get together and pick out the clothes you're going to take on your honeymoon," Angelia replied, trying to appease her mother.

"I can't tonight. We're having dinner with Howard's sister. Perhaps you could come along. You know, you have a whole new family now."

Angelia frowned. "I don't think so, Mother. Your plans have been made, and Howard..."

"Would love to have you there. We didn't invite you only because I know you're usually busy, but if you have the night free, this would be perfect."

"Actually I do have some things I need to do. I was going to put them aside so you and I could spend some time together. I really don't feel like socializing with a lot of people I don't know."

Michelle clucked her tongue in annoyance. "What's the real problem? You just haven't accepted Howard, have you?"

"No. It's not that."

"Then what?"

"I just don't want to get too close too soon," Angelia replied, knowing that her mother wouldn't like the answer.

"You think this marriage is going to fail like the others," Michelle accused.

"I hope not."

"I try to make things work. I really do."

"I know you do." Angelia softened at the hurt expression on her mother's face. "It takes two to make a marriage work, and I know David wasn't much of a family man or a husband."

"You're right there. I wish you'd keep an open mind about Howard. This time I'm marrying for the right reasons. With your father I was blinded by romance and charm. David caught me when I was vulnerable and looking for someone to lean on. But this time it's different. Howard and I understand each other, faults and all. He knows I'm a bit of a scatter-brain. I know he's a little stodgy. But none of that matters, because we really love each other. It's right between us. I feel it in my heart and in my head. That's a first for me.''

Angelia smiled. "You've convinced me. And I envy your confidence. I wish I could trust my own instincts where love is concerned."

"Love? As in Nicholas Hunter?"

"Yes," she conceded. "He's the first man that I've ever really wanted to trust, to believe in. I just like being with him, talking to him."

"And he makes your heart race faster?"

"That, too."

"Sounds like a good combination."

"Sometimes I think yes, sometimes I think no. We're very different and yet in some ways we're very much alike. I'm just afraid I'm being too optimistic about our chances together."

"Well, I say go for it. Nicholas Hunter is a good man. I may not always have the best judgment, but I do have experience on my side."

"Thanks. And for the record, I think Howard is very nice, too," Angelia said quietly, drawing a pleased smile from her mother. "I don't have anything at all against him or you being together. I hope you'll believe that. And as for the rest of his family, just give me a little time to adjust."

"All right. Thank you for saying that. It means a lot to me."

"And you mean a lot to me. Now, get out of here, so I can get my class started on time."

"I'm going. But remember the rehearsal dinner is Friday night at seven."

"Don't worry, I'll be there."

"If you want to bring Mr. Hunter, he's more than welcome."

"I'll keep it in mind, but Nicholas hasn't been too available lately. In fact I think he's trying to avoid me."

"Sounds like love."

"Or a severe case of tangoitis."

Nicholas fiddled with his pen, rifled through his file folders restlessly and then finally sat back in his chair, staring impatiently at the clock on his desk. Five o'clock. He had made it through another day without walking by the ballroom. Of course, he had been tempted. He had even made it as far as the end of the hall, when one of the bellhops had brought him back to his senses with an urgent call to attend to a large group of Japanese businessmen in one of the meeting rooms.

Even though he hadn't actually gone into the ballroom, he couldn't help but notice that Angelia's presence was having an effect on everyone. Her students were always floating through the lobby in leotards and dance wear, drawing curiosity and interest from the other guests. In fact several of the guests wanted to sign up for lessons, something he had never even considered.

And then there was Angelia with her ready, wide smile and her sparkling brown eyes and her contagious sense of fun that had all the bellhops drooling over her and even the crustiest of his managers unbending long enough to personally adjust the air temperature in the ballroom.

Resting his chin on his hands, he stared blankly down at the sleek, polished surface of his mahogany desk. What on earth had he gotten himself into? The land deal in Argentina was turning his entire life upside down. There seemed to be surprises around every corner, and feelings and emotions he had long thought buried kept brimming to the surface.

He found himself smiling at odd times, usually when he was thinking about her. And his deliberately harsh view toward the reality of life was softening as he began to see things through her eyes. He was beginning to want more than just material goods, success and respect. He wanted laughter and love and a pair of dark seductive eyes that wouldn't look at anyone but him.

"Mr. Hunter." His secretary's professional, polite voice rang over the intercom. "Do you need anything else before I go?"

He pushed the button down to reply. "No, thank you, Marilyn. I'll see you tomorrow."

"Oh, by the way, Miss Martinez called again. She wants to know when your next lesson is."

"Thank you. I'll take care of it."

He switched the intercom off and sat quietly, listening to the relentless ticking of the clock. After a moment he picked up his pencil and began to make a list. It was the way he went about every project. Pros on one side. Cons on the other. Then he would make a simple, logical decision.

Angelia paused momentarily as the stereo flipped to the next song. She jogged in place and then began to move, her mind mentally making up steps and moves. The pounding, moving beat of the music made it easy to bend and twist and skip until her heart was beating wildly and her face was flushed with exertion. Still, the conflict in her mind continued to nag at her.

She tried to think about choreography. She wanted a new routine for her advanced aerobics class, one that would stretch her eager students to the limit and at the same time work all the muscle groups. But instead of counting and repeating movements until she had a routine firm in her mind, she just danced. It was the only way she knew how to work through her problems.

Alone in the ballroom with the music and the mirror, she felt free to express herself, to work out the tension that knotted into her shoulders when she thought about her business problems or when she thought about Nicholas.

The man was literally haunting her with his advance-and-retreat behavior. Every time they started to get close, to share something more personal than the weather, he would back off. She knew he was attracted to her; the electricity between them was unmistakable. But it was just as obvious that he didn't want to be attracted. Every time he kissed her he apologized, which was doing nothing for her ego. What did he want from her? More importantly, what did she want from him?

She was so wrapped up in her thoughts that she didn't register the opening of the ballroom door or the startled expression on Nicholas's face as he stood by the wall, captivated by the sight of her.

In a wild purple print leotard, with the light sheen of perspiration on her shoulders and back, she looked sexier than any woman he had ever seen. Her hair, pulled back in a traditional braid, was slowly working its way free, curling in long waves past her shoulder blades. Mentally he added one more item to his pro list and then cleared his throat and walked over to her.

"Nicholas," she gasped in surprise, catching sight of him in the mirror. Her right foot came down hard, and she grimaced at the sudden pain up her arch.

"Are you all right?" he asked as she bent over to rub her foot.

"Fine. You just startled me," she said breathlessly. Standing up straight, her breath caught as the desire flowed between them. What did she want from him? The answer hit her like the jagged edge of a needle across an old record. "What...what are you doing here?"

"Looking for you." He took a step back and loosened his tie at the collar. "I guess we need to talk about the tango."

"The tango...right. Actually we need to do a little more than talk if you're still planning on going through with your performance. I tried to call you, but your secretary said you were busy."

"It's been a hectic week. And I thought you needed time to settle in."

"Yes, but everything is running smoothly now. I'm really happy with our arrangement, and I do want to hold up my end of the bargain. So, whenever you're ready."

He sighed and raised his hands in defeat. "I guess I'm ready now. Shall we go?"

"Pardon me?"

"To my house for the tango lesson."

She looked at him in confusion. "We don't need to go to your house. We can do it right here."

"And take a chance that one of my staff might walk in? No, I don't think so."

"You're afraid they'll find out you're a closet tango dancer?" she asked with a smile. "You know, there's really nothing shameful about the dance."

"I'm not so sure about that," he said dryly. "I've seen the way you move, Angelia, and there's nothing G-rated about it."

"What do you mean?"

"You know what I mean."

The intensity in his voice sent a wave of heat through her body, successfully blocking any attempt at a retort. She simply couldn't think of anything to say to such a blatant comment.

"Why don't we go to my house?" he repeated with a swiftly curving smile.

"Your house," she echoed, not liking the sudden sparkle in his eyes.

"Yes, we can be alone there. Just you and me and the tango."

Her heart spun at the deliberateness of his words, innocent on the surface but distinctly challenging.

"What do you say?"

She didn't know what to say. Damn the man. Why couldn't he be consistent? One minute he was moody and irritable, the next he was teasing and making sexy innuendos. She was beginning to wonder just what his real personality was.

"Angelia, you're stalling. I know because it's a tactic I've used more than once."

"I'm not stalling, I'm thinking. I have to stop by the bridal salon to try on my dress. Maybe we should reschedule our lesson for tomorrow or the next day."

"Much as I would love to reschedule it into the year 2000, I'm afraid we're going to have to keep going. We only have a little over a week before we go to Argentina. How long will your fitting take?"

"Fifteen minutes, if they're not busy."

"Then I'll meet you at my house. Have you eaten?"

"Not yet."

"Why don't I pick up some Chinese food on the way home?"

"All right. But don't go to too much trouble. I'm really not that hungry."

"You will be," he predicted, waving goodbye as he walked out the door.

Chapter Seven

Hungry? She was starving, but not for food. Caught up in Nicholas's arms, she wanted to reach out and stroke the light stubble along his cheekbone. She wanted to take her fingers and trace the irritated line of his mouth as he concentrated on counting and making the right steps. But she held back, reminding herself that she was his teacher and this was just a dance.

His arm around her waist tightened as he staunchly executed the steps. The hardness of his chest against her breasts made her want to linger in the embrace instead of making the usual movements to and from his body. She couldn't concentrate. The incessant pounding of her heart was getting in the way of her counts.

She wondered if he was feeling the same way, but incredibly his expression was still guarded. She couldn't believe that he could be oblivious to the strong undercurrents of attraction flowing back and forth between them. But there was no time left to analyze. As the music stopped, Nicholas's foot caught the corner of his carpet, and they stumbled together, finally falling against the back of the couch.

Nicholas stared into her eyes, his cheeks flushed from exertion, his blue eyes bright with desire. He knew. He felt it, too.

She should be moving, getting to her feet, instead of lying sprawled against his chest, but she couldn't move; she wanted him to kiss her. He lowered his head slowly, his lips coming to rest against hers in a light, tender touch. Her mouth opened under his, and he kissed her more deeply, passionately, his hands moving down the length of her spine and back up to her neck, his fingers burying themselves in her hair.

When he finally pulled away, they were both breathless, but almost immediately the shutter clicked down in his eyes. After a muttered curse he helped her to her feet.

"We should have moved the carpet out of the way," he said jerkily.

"It was my fault, too. I wasn't looking."

She turned to him and saw the uneasiness she felt reflected in his eyes. As much as she wanted to ask him what he was feeling, she held back. "I'm hungry. Maybe we should eat now," she said finally. "Did you pick something up on the way home? Or shall I rummage through the refrigerator and find something to make?"

"It's all taken care of," he replied with relief. "It's in the kitchen. After you."

"Thanks," she said, resolving to get through the rest of the evening with as much dignity as she could muster.

Once they reached the kitchen, she began opening the cartons of Chinese food laid out on the counter while he reached for plates and silverware. The kitchen clatter eased the tension between them, and after they set up the meal, they began to eat.

"How long have you been dancing?" Nicholas asked a short time later.

"Since I was born. My mother was a dancer. She actually performed on Broadway. That's where my parents met. She was dancing in the chorus of a show, and he came to see her, and they fell in love. At least that's the story they always told."

"It sounds very romantic," he said dryly.

"I used to think so. Of course, it didn't last." She paused. "My father was a businessman, very much like you. But he did like to dance. In fact one of my strongest memories is of him and my mother doing the tango at a private party they had. I remember thinking that they were the most beautiful couple on earth."

"What happened?"

"I don't know." She met his eyes steadily. "My mother has never been able to explain, and I haven't heard from my father since the day we left."

Nicholas stared back at her somberly. "Why?"

"Apparently he didn't care enough to keep in touch." She shrugged her shoulders. "That's why I was reluctant to agree to your plan. I'm not sure I want to go back to Argentina."

"You don't have to see him," he pointed out logically. "He may not even still be there."

"That's true. But it's not just the idea of seeing him that bothers me, it's everything else, the countryside, the buildings, seeing the places that I remember as a child. Everyone says that you can't go back. I'm beginning to think the same thing. If it wasn't for the dance school, I don't think I would.''

"So you're willing to do it for your business?''

"Yes, because the school is more than just a business to me. It's like a home. For the past ten years it has been the one thing in my life that is stable. We used to change apartments almost every year, moving up or down depending on my mother's income. But the school was always there. It was the one place I could be free to just be Angelia Martinez, a girl of mixed heritage, a little bit different than everyone else. But at a dance school, being different is a good thing.''

Nicholas shook his head in concern. "I don't know, Angelia. It sounds like you're thinking about your school with too much emotion and not enough realism. What does the profit-and-loss statement look like? What is the bottom line?''

"Okay and not so good,'' she retorted. "And our accountant has already told me how difficult it will be to make a good living with the school as it is now. But I don't intend to let a little negative thinking set me back. I can make the school whatever I want. It just depends on how hard I'm willing to work.''

"It depends on a lot of other things as well, the market, the pricing, the interest of the local community.''

"Are you trying to depress me?''

"I don't think I could,'' he said with a smile. "You're an incurable optimist.''

"And why not?''

"You can take some hard falls when your head is in the clouds and you're not looking down at the ground."

"But I'll have a better view along the way."

He tilted his head at her, acknowledging her point. "Agreed."

"Haven't you looked at a few clouds, Nicholas? I can't imagine how you could build an empire as large as yours without doing a little bit of dreaming."

"I've done my share, but I always try to make the dreams fit into a realistic picture. And there are a few I've had to give up along the way because of that."

"But this land in Argentina isn't one of them."

"Not yet."

"What about the tango?"

"What about it?"

"This is the third time we've tried to have a lesson and so far we haven't gotten past twenty minutes."

He dropped his eyes and helped himself to some more rice. "You were the one who said you were hungry."

"Right." She studied his bent head for a long moment, wondering how they were going to break down the wall between them.

"More almond chicken?" he asked blandly.

"No, thanks."

"You sure?"

"Yes."

After a moment she sighed so loudly he looked up at her in surprise. "Something wrong?"

"Yes. You can't keep dodging me on this. We're never going to be able to dance in front of your friends if we don't practice a little, get to know each other better. The tango is more than just steps and counts, it's about emotion, feelings, expressing yourself with your body."

"We're talking about a dance."

"Of course we are," she said crossly as he tried to brush aside her words. "The tango is communication between a man and woman, two independent people challenging each other to dance in a way that expresses the way they feel about themselves, about life...about love."

"And I'm not doing that?" he asked facetiously.

"No."

"Good. Because I don't want to bare my soul in front of a roomful of people. And I don't think you want to, either."

"I do it all the time."

"You do not," he denied. "The woman who danced with Ricardo in the studio is not the real Angelia. You put on a face. You give the people what they want. That's all I'm trying to do."

She looked at him for a long moment, stunned by his perception. "That's true to a certain extent. But I still dance with feeling no matter who my partner is. If I'm happy, I want to show it. If I'm sad, same thing. Otherwise I'd look like a robot out there."

"Fortune cookie, Angelia?"

She sighed. "I give up. Yes, I'll take a cookie."

He handed her a cookie and watched as she silently read the fortune. "Is it good news or bad?"

She rolled her eyes. "Watch your step, everything is not as it seems." She tossed the paper down in disgust. "What does yours say?"

"I'm not having one," he replied. "I don't think I can risk it."

"There's that cautious side again."

"Yes," he said agreeably. "I'm superstitious as hell and I don't trust anybody. Do you want more coffee?"

"What?" she asked, trying to keep up with the constant shift in his conversation.

"Coffee? Do you want more?"

"No, thanks. I'd like to hear more about you, why you don't feel you can trust anyone."

"It's a boring story. I think I'll have a beer. Can I get you anything else?"

"Maybe we should think about resuming our dance lesson," she said with a touch of irritation in her voice. She didn't like the way he controlled the conversation to suit himself, but at the moment there wasn't anything she could do about it.

"On a full stomach?" he asked with a frown. "That can't be good for the digestion."

"You have a hundred and one excuses, Nick."

"Come on, didn't your mother tell you to wait an hour before dancing?"

"That was swimming, not dancing."

"Same thing."

"Then I guess I might as well go home."

"Damn, it's nine o'clock," he said abruptly, his gaze switching to the clock. "There was a show I wanted to watch. It's one of those murder mysteries with Columbo. I love that guy."

"Is that my cue to leave?"

"No." He smiled. "I don't think either one of us is in the mood to do any more dancing tonight. But you could stay and watch the movie with me. We could get to know each other better, like you were saying."

It was an olive branch, and she knew it. After a moment she nodded her head in agreement. "I do like mysteries. Sure. Why not? Where is the television?"

"I have a big screen in the family room. We can watch it in there."

She walked out of the kitchen into the large, country-style family room set at the back of the house. The entertainment center was completely modern and sophisticated, and the big-screen television would not have even fit into her apartment. The differences between them were beginning to make the Grand Canyon look small.

"Good, it's just starting," Nicholas announced, breaking into her thoughts. He picked up the remote control and patted the seat on the couch next to him. "Make yourself comfortable."

Chapter Eight

Comfortable? Curled up on the couch with Nicholas's hard thighs touching lightly against hers was making her feel distinctly uncomfortable. The mystery on the television was a good one, but even so, her thoughts kept drifting to the man sitting next to her. He was such a puzzle, moody and then teasing, joking and then serious. Just when he seemed to relax a little bit, his eyes would darken and he would suddenly snap the walls back up in place, keeping her firmly on the other side. What was he hiding? Why did everyone seem to have so many secrets?

Her mother didn't want to talk about Argentina, and Nicholas didn't want to talk about much of anything. She, on the other hand, wanted to have a deep heart-to-heart with both of them. She had been a coward for too long, letting her mother slide by with her flimsy excuses and Nicholas change the subject every other minute. Despite his avoidance, she sensed that he needed to talk to somebody. But he didn't trust her, and she didn't know how to convince him otherwise.

"Nicholas," she started.

"Shh, this is the good part."

She sighed and waited for the commercial. "Nicholas, I really think we should talk."

"About what?" he asked, flipping the remote through twenty-seven stations before returning to the movie.

"Maybe about what happened when we were dancing," she said boldly, smiling with satisfaction at his involuntary flinch.

"You mean when you tripped me and then kissed me?"

"I don't think that's what happened," she said dryly.

"Next commercial. Columbo is back on."

"This is a repeat. You must have seen it already."

"I don't think so. Let's watch."

Angelia settled back into the couch with a disgruntled frown. She wasn't getting anywhere this way; she might as well watch the movie. Twenty minutes later she found herself engrossed in the story unfolding on the screen, and both she and Nick looked up in surprise when the doorbell rang.

"I'll see who that is."

"Hope I'm not interrupting anything," Martin said cheerfully as he followed Nicholas back into the family room.

"No, of course not," she replied.

Martin made himself comfortable in the reclining chair and then turned to face Angelia. "How are the tango lessons coming along?"

"Slowly. Very slowly."

"Don't ask her," Nicholas warned. "She just gave me a lecture."

"No kidding? What are you doing wrong? Stepping on her feet?"

"I think it has something to do with my facial expression and eye contact."

"It's more than that," Angelia protested. "You have to dance with emotion, not like an automated robot."

Martin laughed at the description. "Sounds just like you, Nick."

"Yeah, well, I don't really care what I look like as long as it makes Juan Carlos sign on the dotted line."

"That's what I wanted to talk to you about."

Angelia looked from one to the other as both of their expressions turned serious. "I have to get going," she interjected.

"All right," Nicholas agreed. "I'll walk you out."

She nodded and got to her feet. "Nice to see you again, Mr. Hennessey."

He tipped his head. "Always a pleasure."

She walked down the hallway to the front door with Nicholas following behind her.

"We'll set up another lesson tomorrow," he said as she paused and put on a lightweight sweater.

"Whatever you want, Nick." She smiled back at him knowingly, and he grinned in return. "I guess I should go."

"Angelia," he said as she started to turn around. "Tonight was nice." He leaned over and kissed her lightly on the lips, breaking it off before she could even think of taking it further. "Good night."

"Night," she muttered, walking blindly out the door.

He shut the door behind her and stared blankly at the solid oak panel, wondering why he had kissed her. The brief taste only made him want more. He should have left well enough alone. Damn. He walked slowly back to the family room.

Martin was busy changing the channels, using the remote control with an expression of pure joy on his face.

"Find something you like?" Nicholas asked.

"No sports for another four minutes."

"Good. Then use the time to tell me why you're here."

Martin raised an eyebrow. "Did I interrupt something?"

"What do you want?"

"First of all, Juan Carlos called to confirm that we will be arriving a week from Saturday. He's planning to have us over to dinner on Sunday night, and then you can do your infamous tango act."

"Great. Did he say anything about our report?"

"He loved it. Said you have wonderful writers on your staff, but he still wants to see you dance."

"I think the old man is enjoying this."

"You can bet on it," Martin said with a laugh. "I also came by because I need the Penrose file, and I want to take a look at it tonight. You must have it here, because I looked everywhere at the office. We have a meeting with them tomorrow morning, remember? Just in case the Argentina deal doesn't go down."

"Right." He walked over to where his briefcase was lying against the couch, and as he bent over to pick it up, he caught a trace of Angelia's perfume. The knot in his stomach tightened. Stop it. Just stop it, he told himself firmly. She's gone, and it's better that way. She wants too much from you.

He forced himself to open the briefcase and with an effort, fingered through the files until he found the Penrose file. "Here it is." He handed it to Martin.

"Thanks. I guess everything is in order, then. I'll pick you up at eight."

"Fine. I'll be ready."

"Good. Now that we have that out of the way, let's talk about—Angelia. Is she going to go to Argentina with you?"

"Yes, I already told you that. Is there a problem?"

"Not for me."

"What does that mean?"

"We've known each other a long time, Nick."

"So what?"

"So, I know you choose your women very discriminately, and Angelia just doesn't fit the bill. She's too passionate, too sexy and definitely too—"

"I don't know what you're talking about," Nicholas interrupted. "And she's not my woman, she's my dance teacher."

"Right, and you were sure doing a lot of dancing, sitting in front of the television in the dark."

"We were relaxing, not that it's any of your business."

Martin held up a hand in apology. "It's not. But I just wanted to say that for once I approve. I like to see you loosening up a little bit. You used to be a hell of a lot more fun, but the last few years you've gotten way too intense."

"And I've made us both a lot of money."

"But that's not all there is to life."

"I don't hear you complaining."

"I'm not. I've always enjoyed money, but some things are more important. I'd like to see you find someone that you can care about, and I think Angelia fits the bill."

"Thanks for the advice. But Angelia and I are not involved. Now, don't you have to be going?"

"I'm leaving, don't sweat it." He paused at the doorway. "But you might want to wipe the lipstick off your mouth. It's definitely not your color."

Nicholas took an angry swipe at his mouth with the back of his hand and then sat back down and tried futilely to concentrate on the television set.

"Mr. Hunter, we have a major uprising going on in the hotel lobby."

Nicholas looked at his secretary in surprise. They had been working quietly together all morning, but now her usual unflappable manner was definitely missing. Her blond hair was drifting out of its well-kept bun, and her cheeks were flushed a bright red. "What's going on?"

"There's a male strip show in the ballroom."

"What?" he thundered.

"About a dozen of the most glorious males you've ever seen," she added excitedly. "They went right through the lobby, paraded around the pool and then up the stairs to the ballroom, taking half of our female guests with them. The women are now crowding the hallway hoping to get a glimpse inside the ballroom. Security is trying to get rid of them, but they won't budge," she said as Nicholas jumped to his feet. "What are you going to do?"

"I'm going to kill her. Dancers are respectable people, she tells me. You won't even notice we're here, she says. I knew I shouldn't have trusted her," he muttered to himself as he stalked out to the elevator and impatiently pushed the buttons.

When the door opened on the mezzanine level, Nicholas was struck dumb. His secretary hadn't been kidding when she said the floor was packed with females. They came in all shapes and sizes, from sixty to sixteen and in varying stages of dress. Some had obviously come directly from the pool area, not bothering to follow the rules about appropriate dress and attire. Others looked like they had stepped out of one of the various business meetings. He swore to himself, rehearsing what he was going to say to Angelia when he caught up with her.

He pushed his way through the crowd of women, trying to smile pleasantly, but when one of the girls asked if he was going to strip, he turned beet red and fled to the door. The security guard pushed it open for him and shut it firmly behind him. Once inside, he leaned against the door, catching his breath and trying to get a handle on what exactly was going on. There were at least ten men lined up in two rows of five, ten pairs of eyes staring fixedly at Angelia's slender figure in hot pink leotards and a purple T-shirt.

"What the hell is going on?" he demanded, repeating himself as the music coming from the stereo obviously blocked out his words. He strode forward, putting a rough hand on Angelia's shoulder, swinging her around to face him.

She looked up at him in amazement. "Nicholas, you're interrupting my class."

"And you're interrupting my life, not to mention what you're doing to my hotel. Can't you hear the screaming out there?"

"What?" she asked, putting a hand to her ear.

He shook his head and walked over to the stereo, yanking the cord out of the wall with a resounding screech. "That noise," he repeated.

Angelia turned toward the closed doors, suddenly aware of the pandemonium going on outside. "What's the problem? Is there an emergency or something?"

One of the men started laughing, and a couple of others looked at each other knowingly. Nicholas followed it all with a grim smile. "Are these your students?"

"Yes."

"Don't they need to wear a few more clothes?"

Angelia looked at the bare-chested men and shrugged her shoulders. "It's hot in here."

"Angelia," he yelled. "They walked through the hotel like that, across the front lobby, around the pool, through the exercise room. There are about a hundred women out there, trying to get inside. What's going on?"

"I don't know." She turned to face the group of smirking young men. "Okay, whose idea was it to go strutting through the hotel?"

"Vinnie's," one of the guys called out. "We were just trying to drum up some business."

"For what?" Nicholas asked with dangerous quiet.

Angelia cleared her throat, suddenly realizing the depth of her problem. "They dance at the Van der Kellen Club in Beverly Hills."

"The Van der Kellen Club," he repeated. "They're strippers, right?"

"Male dancers," she corrected, "at least while they're here. I'm teaching them steps, that's it."

"Yeah, right."

"Don't you believe me?"

"I don't much care at the moment. I just want them out of here."

"Hey, we've got twenty minutes left," one of the guys protested. "You can't cut us off early without a refund."

"He's right. Please, can't we just finish the class?" Angelia pleaded. "I really can't afford to do any more refunds."

"What am I going to do about the women? They're blocking the hallway and the fire exits. You're turning this hotel upside down."

"I'm sorry. Why don't you let them in? They can watch and get autographs, and then everyone will go back to what they were doing, no harm done," she added hopefully.

"No harm done," he repeated incredulously. "Fine. Have it your way." He walked over to the door and opened it, instinctively stepping back from the mad crush of women. He looked at the older security guard in disgust. "Let them in, Fred. There's no point in keeping them out here."

A round of applause greeted his statement as the crowd pushed past him into the ballroom. When the last woman was inside, he shut the door to the ballroom and stared grimly at the now-empty hallway.

"Do you want me to wait?" Fred asked respectfully.

"No, you can go back to your usual post. We won't be having a repeat of this again."

"I couldn't quite believe my eyes. Never saw such an ogling crowd of women in my life. Things have sure changed since I was a young man. Never would see a woman coming on to a man like that. Course, I don't recall too many men walking around hotels half-naked."

"I think I must be getting old, too," Nicholas agreed. "And no matter how old I get, I don't come any closer to understanding women."

Fred patted him on the back. "Don't try to understand, Mr. Hunter. Just enjoy them. That's what life is all about. See you later."

"Yeah. Thanks."

Fred paused. "Oh, and don't blame that pretty Miss Martinez for all this. She was inside the ballroom the whole time. I don't think she knew anything about the antics those boys pulled."

"I'll keep that in mind," Nicholas replied, storming back to his office.

Angelia pulled her hair back into a ponytail and faced herself in the ballroom mirror. She was feeling restless and edgy after the day's events, wondering what she could possibly do to make things better.

Instead of her usual optimism, she felt depressed. Nicholas had been furious with her. And when she had seen the gaggle of women that burst into the ballroom, she had felt some anger herself. But it wasn't her fault. She hadn't known that the guys were going to show themselves off at the hotel. If she had, she would certainly have put a stop to it.

Nicholas probably wouldn't believe her. He was always looking for reasons to distrust her, and this was going to be marked as a black strike against her. She felt an incredible heaviness in her heart at the thought. She didn't want to be angry with Nicholas. She wanted to be friends, close friends, best friends, maybe even . . .

With a sigh she pulled one leg up behind her in a stretch, relishing the ache in her muscles. She wanted to feel pain. At least that was real, concrete, not like the strange feelings that were continually hitting her. She felt on edge, with her emotions right on the surface. It didn't seem to take much to make her laugh or cry. Everything was just brimming over, ready to spill at the first unexpected movement.

She wondered if Nicholas was still planning on his tango lesson that night or if he was too angry with her to continue. No, he had too much at stake to let something this small stop him. He would keep going, and so would she.

She just needed to get rid of the tension. She needed to dance.

Rolling her neck, she closed her eyes and began to relax. Music. She needed music to move by, to escape. She flipped on a tape filled with pulsating Latin rhythms. It was the music that fit her best when she was feeling restless and upset. Slowly she began to move, and then her steps picked up, faster and faster as she whirled across the floor and back again. She imagined herself in another place and time, a silky black dress, a red rose in her hair, a handsome lover in the shadows, beckoning to her.

It was just a dream, but for a moment it was just what she needed.

* * *

"We need to set some ground rules," Nicholas said sharply as she followed him into his living room later that night.

"I know. First I want to apologize." She turned to face him, but as she did so, the words fled from her mind. His hair was dark and deliciously rumpled from what had obviously been a recent shower, and his eyes were as blue as the twilight sky outside. He was a wonderful-looking man despite the frown and wariness in his eyes.

"Go on," he prodded, folding his arms across his chest.

"You want to hear the whole thing, right?"

"Every word."

"I would never do anything to jeopardize your business. Despite the fact that I'm a dancer, I do understand what is appropriate in business and what is not."

"Really?"

"Yes, really," she snapped. "I just didn't anticipate that the guys would walk through your hotel that way. When they come to the studio, they arrive in sweats and leave the same way. I had no idea they were going to create such chaos. If I had, I would have stopped it."

"How can you teach men like that?" he asked curiously, then shrugged his question away. "Forget I asked that."

"They're dancers," she said simply. "Yes, they do take off their clothes, at least some of them, but I'm not involved with that. I'm not making moral judgments on them. They come to me to learn how to dance. That's it.''

"Is it? They were staring at you like kids in a candy store.''

She stared at him in amazement. Was that jealousy in his voice or just irritation for having upset his normal routine? "What do you mean by that?''

"Nothing. Let's just forget it,'' he said roughly. "Just make sure it doesn't happen again.''

"It won't. You have my word. That particular group has been instructed to come in full clothing and without any more nonsense.''

"Right.'' He walked around the room switching on lamps, successfully obliterating the cozy light of dusk. "So, what now? Any more surprises?''

She hesitated and then decided she might as well talk to him while she had the chance. "A few of your guests did come by this afternoon.''

"I already know that.''

"Not the women,'' she said abruptly. "You have a group of senior citizens staying at your hotel for the next two weeks. I believe they're on some sort of a package tour.''

"Were they upset by something?''

"No,'' she replied with a wry twist. "They were excited to see me teaching the tango, and they wondered if they could take some lessons while they're at the hotel.''

"No. Absolutely not.'' He shook his head hard and fast. "You are not going to get my guests involved in your classes just because you need to drum up business.''

"I'm not doing that," she protested. "They came to me. What would be the harm?"

"Just leave it alone."

"No. I don't understand your attitude. You act like dancing is a sin or something."

"Look, I just agreed to let you use the ballroom. I don't want you mixing everything up."

His words were edged with emotion, and when she looked into his eyes, she knew they were talking about more than just dancing. "Is that what I'm doing?"

"After today, I'd say yes."

"Maybe you're doing the same thing to me," she suggested.

He turned away. "If they want to dance, sign them up."

"Thank you." She took a deep breath and smiled cheerily. "So, are you ready for another shot at the tango?"

"In a few minutes. Do you want something first?"

"No, I think we've already been through this routine, Nick."

"I don't want you to call me Nick. My name is Nicholas."

"What is the matter with you? You've been yelling at me since I got here."

He looked at her and sighed. "I'm tired. I don't think this is a good idea, not tonight. We'll just end up in an argument."

"We only have one more week."

"Don't remind me."

"All right. I'm kind of tired myself." She picked up her purse and walked back to the front door. "I am sorry."

"I know you are," he said huskily.

"We'll be good, Nicholas. You won't even know we're there."

He shook his head, his lips turning into a rare smile. "I doubt that, Angelia."

"Oh, one other thing. I was wondering if you were still interested in going to my mother's wedding."

"Saturday at five, right?"

"Yes. I know it's Valentine's Day and you probably have other plans."

"Not really. I've never been big on Valentine's Day."

She could believe that. Sentiment and romance were hardly his strong suit. "Then you're free?"

"I suppose."

"Don't let me twist your arm."

"Now you're snapping at me," he replied with a frown. "Why?"

"I just don't want you to do anything that you don't want to do."

"That's not usually a problem, Angelia."

"No, I guess it's not," she agreed, facing him with a steady but determined glance. "If you'd like to come, you're welcome. If not, it's no big deal."

"I'll come," he decided. "Can I pick you up?"

She shook her head. "No, I have to be there early. It would be best if we met at Howard's house."

He nodded, and they stared at each other again for a long, tense moment.

"I'll see you then," she said finally.

Nicholas watched her go with mixed feelings. He wanted to call her back, to invite her in, even if he had to dance the damn tango. But he knew it would be a mistake. They were both too edgy, too tense. He wouldn't be able to keep his hands off of her, and then she would want to talk, and the last thing he wanted to do was talk. Thank God, they only had one more week before Argentina. Then he could put her out of his life for good.

Chapter Nine

"You look beautiful," Michelle said wistfully. She came up behind Angelia to stare at the reflection of mother and daughter in the mirror.

Angelia smiled. "I'm supposed to say that. I don't think you've ever looked quite as radiant as you do today."

"That's because I'm so happy. The only thing that would make me happier would be to see you walking down the aisle."

"Oh, please, that's a long way away."

"Is it? I was hoping..."

"Some day, Mother, but not now."

Michelle nodded, fingering the sapphire heart in her necklace. "You've grown into a beautiful woman. Strong and confident. I think maybe you're ready to go to Argentina."

Angelia whirled around in surprise. "That's a strange thing for you to say."

"Maybe I've been wrong to try to protect you. But it's your decision now, and I'm here if you need me."

"Thank you. I'll always need you."

"I haven't been much of a mother to you. I let you down so many times when you were in school, missing your plays and forgetting to bake the cookies for the PTA bake sale."

Angelia laughed, hugging her lightly as she did so. "Will you stop it? You were a great mom."

"But I didn't give you a stable home, a traditional life."

"I'm not a traditional person," Angelia replied. "You gave me love. That's all I needed. Now, it's time for you to give Howard some of that love."

"Yes, but sometimes I wish . . ."

"What?"

"That I could go to him as a young woman, full of innocence and passion, not a middle-aged woman with a rather disreputable past."

"You're not disreputable, and sometimes I think you're more innocent than I am. It's funny, because Nicholas Hunter thinks I'm a dreamer, but I always thought you were the dreamer."

"I guess I always have been, which probably wasn't fair to you. While I was making my dreams, you were taking care of Michael and making sure we had food in the refrigerator. You were dependable and strong. Maybe Nicholas just hasn't seen that side of you."

"I don't think he wants to see that side."

"Because he's afraid of love," Michelle said wisely. "It can be frightening, but I think it's worth it."

Angelia smiled. "So do I. And now I think it's time for you to take that last scary step."

Michelle nodded, her eyes misting with tears. "Wish me luck."

"I don't think you're going to need luck this time." Angelia walked over and opened the door. "Shall we go? Howard is waiting."

A nontraditional blend of flute and clarinet accompanied Angelia as she walked down the long spiral staircase in Howard's home into the living room, where an intimate crowd of about thirty people were waiting for the bride. Her step faltered only once when her gaze came to rest on Nicholas's tall, straight figure. He was exceedingly handsome in his black tuxedo and starchy white shirt, and her heart swelled at the sight of him.

He smiled as she passed him, a curiously unguarded look that remained with her throughout the solemn but joyful candlelight ceremony. After her mother and Howard exchanged vows, the dining room was opened and they indulged in a long, drawn-out dinner reception filled with champagne toasts and plenty of joyous anecdotes about the two lovers.

Nicholas was quietly charming throughout most of the evening, chatting with the other guests and generally providing Angelia all the support she could have wished for. He didn't even seem to mind when everyone mistakenly assumed that they were a couple. He just answered their questions with an easy warmth that made her wish they really were a couple.

After dinner they finally had a chance to escape into the garden for a breath of fresh air and some privacy.

"This was a nice evening," Nicholas said as they walked along the terrace. "It was very tasteful, elegant. I liked it."

"So did I." She smiled up at him. "My mother's last wedding wasn't anything like this. It was very ostentatious. I had to walk down a hideously long aisle and wear the fluffiest dress I'd ever seen in my life. It was a production, and I hated every minute of it. But this one was different. I think the marriage will be, too."

Nicholas raised his eyebrows but didn't say anything.

"You don't think too much of marriage, do you?" she asked abruptly, studying his profile with an intense longing to understand him better.

"I guess not. I certainly don't have any personal experience to base it on. My parents were never married."

"I'm sorry."

"It was a long time ago. My father didn't hang around much longer than it took to conceive me, and my mother left me at the convent when I was four years old. She told me she would be back." His eyes clouded over. "And I believed her."

Angelia was filled with emotion at his simple, painful statement. No wonder he found it so difficult to trust people.

"But she never came back. I don't know where she is now. I don't much care. I've put it behind me."

"Not entirely," she replied. "But I think I understand."

He turned to look at her, his strong jaw curving into a small smile. "Maybe you do at that. But my situation is not the same as yours, and I have resolved my feelings. Maybe there's still some bitterness, but I've come to terms with it."

"No, you haven't. You won't come to terms with it until you let yourself trust someone, love someone."

"I'm not sure I can do that," he said huskily. "I don't think love is anything like it's cracked up to be. Most of my friends are divorced or in marriages that are convenient but hardly passionate. I don't think I'm missing anything."

"I do," she said firmly. "I may come from a broken home, but I still believe in love and marriage and the whole idea of a family."

"That's because you're a dreamer, and I'm a realist."

"I think the two can go together."

"So, what kind of future do you see for yourself—theoretically speaking, of course?"

She thought for a moment and then slowly began to speak. "I see a roaring fire on a cold winter day, and a loving family gathered around a big oak table in the kitchen. I hear the laughter of children, maybe even a few squabbles, and I can even smell the aroma of an apple pie baking in the oven." She laughed at her fantasy. "Yes, I want a husband and a family and love."

"What about your dance school?"

"I want that, too."

"It's going to be tough to run a dance school from your kitchen."

"I won't always be in the kitchen."

"For your husband's sake, I certainly hope not." He grinned as she made a face.

"I won't always be in the bedroom, either."

"So you're going to be a businesswoman and a wife and a mother. In other words, you want everything."

"Just like you."

"No, I want the business, nothing else."

"Oh, come on, doesn't a cozy kitchen on a cold winter day with a loving family sound wonderful to you?"

"For about thirty seconds. And I don't care much for apple pie," he said mockingly, trying to ignore the deep yearning in his gut that her words had created.

"So, make it cherry or blueberry or better yet, coconut cream."

"Stop, you're making me hungry."

"Seriously, Nick. I know it sounds like I want everything, but that's not really the case. I don't need money or fame or power."

"Like me, you mean."

"I don't believe that's all you want."

"Why not?"

"Because it's too cold-blooded, too calculating."

"I've heard worse insults in my life."

"Stop it. Stop trying to be the ruthless businessman. I don't buy it."

"Well, you should, because that's what I am." His jaw tightened suddenly. "We're not the same kind of people, Angelia. The sooner you realize that, the better."

"Why are you trying so hard to make me believe the worst of you?" She took a step closer to him, fingering the lapel of his jacket with a mischievous smile. "Am I getting too close?"

His gut tightened in an annoyingly familiar reaction to her touch. "You don't know what you're getting yourself into. That's the problem. You don't think, you just jump in and hope for the best."

"That's not true. Maybe I'm a little more spontaneous than you are, but I do consider the consequences of my actions."

"Really?" His hand captured her roving fingers,
stilling them against his chest so that she could hear
the pounding beat of his heart through his white silk
shirt. "Then you know what you're doing right now?"
he asked with deadly quiet.

She let out a small gasp of air as he pulled her body
against his and tilted her face upward until their lips
were only inches apart. "I think so," she murmured,
her heart racing with anticipation. "What about
you?"

"I think..." He traced the outline of her jaw with
his finger, his blue eyes darkening with desire. "I think
I'm going crazy."

The last word ended in a growl against her lips as he
kissed her with a passion that surprised her. No gentle touch, no carefully thought out caress, but the raw
edge of desire and longing. She opened her mouth as
his tongue danced intimately with hers in an erotic
movement that had her clinging to him, mindlessly
hoping that the moment could go on forever.

But the need for breath finally drove them apart,
and Angelia turned blindly away. She felt suddenly
lost without his arms around her, and confused by the
rush of emotions his kiss had stirred up. Maybe he was
right. Maybe she wasn't ready for the consequences.

"Angelia," he said softly. "Are you all right?"

"Fine. I'm fine," she replied hastily, summoning up
a smile. "You pack quite a punch."

"So do you."

His words dropped into another awkward silence.

"Do you want to go inside now?" he asked finally.

She stared at him and then burst out laughing.

"What's so funny?" he asked warily.

"You. I think you're the master at retreat."

"If you want an apology..."

"No, thank you."

"Our game just got a little out of hand."

"It's more than a game between us," she replied.

"Well, there is the tango."

"And the attraction we feel for one another."

"You're a beautiful woman, passionate in everything that you do. What happened was just a natural progression." His words came out in clipped, precise tones, and her temper flared.

"Do you think I kiss everyone the way I kissed you?"

He stared into her angry eyes and tried to smile. "That's a loaded question."

"It's because I'm a dancer. You think I have no morals."

"I never said that."

"And my mother getting married for the third time doesn't exactly help my image, does it?"

"You're putting words in my mouth." Nicholas sighed at the hurt tone in her voice. She was as sensitive as she was passionate. She was also beautiful and warm and caring. He felt as if he had just stepped on a butterfly. "I think you're a wonderful person, so full of life that you make everyone around you happy. And your mother's marriages have nothing to do with you. I don't hold you accountable for her actions. Hell, it's not even any of my business how many times your mother gets married."

"Then what is it? Why do you kiss me and then back away?"

"I'm trying to be sensible about this. Sure, there's an attraction here. You're a woman. I'm a man. One plus one equals two. Sparks and fuel equal combustion." He snapped his fingers to emphasize his point.

She shook her head in anger. "Stop trying to turn our relationship into a mathematical equation. We're people with emotions and feelings and intangibles. No matter how much you try to deny that, it's true. Our relationship grows more complicated every day. There's nothing simple about it."

"I agree with that. You don't play the game like anyone else I know."

"That's because I'm not playing. One day you're going to realize that what you and I could have together would be pretty incredible." She stared up at him, her brown eyes earnest, challenging but wary. "But for now, maybe you should get us some champagne."

He opened his mouth to say something and then changed his mind. What could he say? It had been a mistake to kiss her. He told himself that every time it happened, but when he was with her, he couldn't seem to keep his hands off of her. They just needed some time apart, some space between them so they could get their priorities in order. Swearing to himself, he pushed his way back into the party in search of two glasses of hopefully cooling champagne.

Twenty-four hours without Nicholas Hunter wasn't nearly enough to get him out of her mind, but it was a start, Angelia thought as she walked into the hotel early Monday morning. She had five more days before they left for Argentina. She would simply keep things businesslike. And once they got back, she would never have to see him again.

Lord! What a depressing thought that was. As annoying as he was, as irritating as he could be, she was becoming resigned to the fact that she was hopelessly attracted to him. She tried to tell herself that his logical, analytical, cautious personality would probably drive her crazy, but the truth was that she was much more in tune with those traits than he realized.

Yes, she was passionate. But she was also careful. Her early-childhood rejection had instilled a wariness in her that tempered her spontaneity. She liked to have fun, but she also liked stability, something she had never seen much of in her life. That's why she was clinging to the dance school. It was the one thing in her life with continuity.

But Nicholas didn't see that side of her. He only saw what he wanted to see. And he didn't want to recognize the fact that they could be good friends, that they could have something special together. There was more than just hormones between them; there was an affinity, a yearning for the kind of family love they had both been deprived of. If only she could make him see that. If only she could get him to trust her.

Definitely too many big *ifs* for eight o'clock on a Monday morning, she thought dismally, pushing her way into her office and taking off her raincoat and hat. Her frown caught between her teeth as she turned around and stared at the man sitting behind her desk.

"Mr. Hennessey. What are you doing here?"

"Writing you a note," Martin replied easily. "But now that you're here, I can pass Nick's message on in person. He wants you to meet him for lunch so he can go over the details for the Argentina trip."

"I see," she said slowly, taking a minute to hang up her coat.

"He would have asked you himself, but he's tied up in a meeting downtown until eleven," Martin explained. "And quite frankly I wanted to take the opportunity to talk to you." He got up from her chair as she walked around the side of the desk. "Have a seat."

"Thank you," she said with a smile. "What did you want to talk to me about?"

"You, Nick—the tango."

"There's nothing to say, I'm afraid. We haven't made much progress. In fact I'm not sure we're even going to be able to do this dance by the end of the week."

"Nick is stalling, huh?"

"In a big way."

He grinned at her. "He doesn't like to dance."

"I've noticed."

"In fact he doesn't like to do much of anything that isn't concerned with business."

"I guess that's why he's so successful at what he does. I'm sure it takes up most of his time."

"But it shouldn't," Martin said firmly. "I've known Nick for twelve years now, since we met at UCLA. And he's never taken a breather from pursuing his goals. He's probably the most single-minded person I've ever met." He paused. "Until now."

Angelia raised her eyebrows quizzically. "What are you trying to tell me in a roundabout way, Mr. Hennessey?"

"Call me Martin."

"Go on."

Martin leaned back in the chair across from her desk and smiled. "I like you, Angelia. I guess I just wanted to tell you that I think you and this tango performance are good for Nick. You've got him thinking about things other than work or money, and that's good for him. He hasn't had an easy life."

"He's told me a few things," she admitted. "But I know he's a very private person."

"He is. And I respect that." He paused again. "Just don't let him get to you. All that grumbling and complaining is on the surface. He's a good guy."

She shook her head at him and gave him a dry smile. "If you're trying to matchmake, forget it. Nicholas Hunter and I are as different as night and day."

"I don't think so. But even if you are opposites, who says there's anything wrong with that?" He held up a hand as she started to interrupt. "I know—you probably have a hundred good reasons to stay away from Nick, and he probably has about two hundred of his own. But he still can't stop the look that comes into his eyes when he talks about you, and I don't think you can, either." He got to his feet. "I'll let you get back to work."

"Thank you. What was that about lunch?"

"Oh, I almost forgot. Nick wants you to meet him downstairs in the restaurant for lunch around noon."

She shook her head immediately. "I can't make it. I have to use the hour to run over to the studio and sign off on some work orders for the construction people. I was just going to grab a sandwich on the way."

Martin pursed his lips thoughtfully. "I'll send Nick along with you. That way you can talk on the way over and back and you can both take care of business."

"I don't think Nicholas wants to go all the way over to the dance studio to talk about our trip. Couldn't we do this later?"

"No. Lunch is about the only free hour he has."

"What about tonight or tomorrow?"

"What's the problem?" Martin asked curiously. "Will it bother you if Nick goes along? He's very good with contractors."

"I'm sure he is. But my remodel job is peanuts compared to what he does."

"Maybe so. But he can still help a friend."

Angelia threw up her hands under his persistent arguments. "Fine. Tell him to meet me in the parking lot at noon. I have an orange Volkswagen with the bumper sticker, I'd Rather Be Dancing."

Martin grinned again. "Figures. He'll be there."

"If he's late, I'm leaving," she warned.

"He won't be." He paused at the door. "By the way, I think your dance school has been a great boost for the hotel. I'll be sorry to see you go."

"So will I," Angelia muttered as he shut the door. But she didn't want to think past her trip to Argentina, or the next few weeks when it would no longer be necessary to see Nick. She could handle lunch with him, but severing all ties was going to be a little more difficult.

Chapter Ten

At five minutes before noon, Nicholas was waiting in the parking lot next to her battered car, a resigned smile on his handsome face.

"I see you got my message," she said brightly, trying to quell the pack of butterflies that flew through her stomach every time she saw him. "I'm sorry about lunch, but this is my only free time."

"So Martin said. I don't suppose I could talk you into going in my car?"

"No way. If the contractor sees me drive up in a Mercedes, I have a feeling the price is going to go up."

"What a cynical thing to say."

She made a face and unlocked the car. Reaching over to the passenger side, she pulled up the lock and then hastily cleared away a pile of leotards and tap shoes from the passenger seat.

"Sorry about the mess."

Nicholas settled his long, lean frame into the car and shook his head. "Don't you know that organization reduces stress? It's a scientific fact."

She laughed at his somber tone. "Hogwash. Dancing relieves stress better than anything else I can think of. In fact just thinking of getting organized sends my blood pressure up. Just another one of the major differences between us, I guess."

"That's what I've been trying to tell you."

Shaking her head, she flipped on the radio and punched a series of buttons, finally settling on a station playing golden oldies. Humming under her breath and tapping her knuckles against the steering wheel, she pulled out of the hotel parking lot and drove quickly to the dance studio.

The car stalled three times during the ten-minute drive, and by the time they reached the dance studio, Nicholas was muttering under his breath.

"Why don't you get a decent car?"

"Finances," she responded cheerfully. "New cars cost money."

"Then maybe you should get this one fixed."

"It's fine. It's just a little temperamental... like you."

"But what if it breaks down on you late at night on a deserted road? What then?"

She looked at him in amazement. "You are such a pessimist."

"Realist," he corrected. "You have to think of the possibilities."

"I can't think of everything. I'd go crazy if I tried to do that."

"No, you'd just lessen the possibility of problems."

"I doubt that. Problems seem to follow me around. Like this one," she added as they walked through the front door of the studio. There were boards everywhere and the smell of freshly sanded wood. Stepping over a half-filled toolbox, Angelia called out hello.

"Mr. Timms. Are you here?"

"Miss Martinez. I'm glad you're here." An older man in his late fifties with graying hair and a scraggly beard came forward with a hammer in one hand and a bag of nails in the other. "I need you to sign off on these change orders. As you know, once we opened up the floor, we found a whole host of plumbing problems just waiting to happen. We're going to have to replace your pipes all the way out to the street, and I'm afraid that's going to up your estimate."

Nicholas opened his mouth to question the man further, but to his surprise, Angelia cut him off.

"How much are we talking about?" she asked sharply.

"About two thousand dollars, labor and materials."

She shook her head. "In your estimate you allowed for the possibility of replacing the pipes. I have it right here."

Mr. Timms frowned and then took the paper from her hand. "Then it will be just the labor. Twelve hundred."

"All right. I'm willing to sign off on that change. But I'd like to make sure that the city is going to inspect the plumbing before we replace the floors."

"Definitely," he agreed as she reached into her purse for a pen. "Thanks." He took the signed order from her hand and went back to work in the main studio.

"Do you want to look around with me?" Angelia asked Nicholas as he continued to stare at her thoughtfully. "Is something wrong?"

"No. You handled that beautifully."

"Thanks. I can be tough when I have to be."

"I'm beginning to realize that."

"Good. Then there's hope for you yet." She grinned and tipped her head, motioning for him to follow her. "Come on. Let's go take a look at the progress, and feel free to let me know if you see something I should pay attention to. I can read a contract, but the more intimate details of construction are beyond me."

Nicholas nodded agreeably, but as they walked around, he found himself more and more impressed by Angelia's business sense and more confused than ever about his feelings toward her. The only thing he knew for sure was that the ache in his gut was getting worse and logical rationalizations for keeping their relationship strictly business were beginning to sink under an overwhelming desire to get personal, very personal.

"I guess that's it," she said as they made their way back to the front door. "I think everything is going well. What do you think?"

"It looks good," he admitted. "The work is professional, and the job is running on time. You can't ask for much more than that."

"We have a good contractor. Actually I have Ricardo to thank for that. He did most of the groundwork for me. Are you ready to go back? We can pick up a sandwich on the way."

He nodded, knowing they still hadn't discussed their trip, but at the moment he was having a hard time concentrating on anything remotely related to business.

When they pulled into the parking lot of the hotel, Angelia looked at him inquiringly. "What did you want to talk to me about?"

"We leave for Argentina on Friday. We'll spend Saturday in Buenos Aires and then we'll go down to Juan Carlos's home on Sunday for the performance. We can return on Monday."

"Is that it?"

He sighed, knowing that he hadn't really needed to have lunch with her; he had just wanted to be with her again. Now he'd made a fool of himself. "That's it," he said. "Unless you have some questions?"

She studied him thoughtfully. "Sounds simple enough. I have a feeling you don't want to go any more than I do."

"I want to go, I just don't want to dance. As for the rest, I think when you see the land, you'll understand my fascination with it."

"I wonder if I will. It seems at odds with your personality. Everything is so cut-and-dried with you. I can't believe you're willing to go to such lengths over a piece of land."

"It's very logical. The profits will be tremendous."

"I don't think it's the money that's motivating you. There has to be something more."

"Money is a very good motivator," he argued, opening his door. "It has always worked for me."

"But there's more to it this time, isn't there?" she persisted.

He hesitated. "Maybe. When do you want to go over the tango again?"

"Tonight," she said crisply. "In the ballroom at seven o'clock."

"I already told you that I'm not dancing in this hotel."

"No, you're not. But that senior citizen group I was telling you about is going to learn the tango tonight. I'm hoping you can pick up something from watching them."

"I don't know, Angelia. Why don't we just meet later at my house?"

"Because we're not getting anything done at your house," she argued. "At least this way you can absorb something just by watching, and hopefully the next time we schedule a lesson you won't feel so uncomfortable."

"Fine. I'll meet you at seven," he agreed. "As long as I don't have to dance."

"God forbid."

He shook his head and walked out the door, ignoring her smile and his own needling urge to smile back.

The four couples were all silver-haired and slightly out of shape, but their smiles were beaming and their enthusiasm inspiring, Angelia thought as she began the simple explanation of the tango. Nicholas had yet to arrive, but she had a feeling that when he did, this group was going to help change his thinking.

"Who wants to go first?" she asked.

"Ethel and I do," Arthur Harrison said eagerly. "We used to dance the tango when we were kids, but it's been over twenty years."

"I'm sure it will come right back to you," she replied. "Step this way."

She turned on the music, filling the room with the pulsating rhythms. With a smile she turned to the first couple. "Let's begin."

The Harrisons did surprisingly well, following her example with barely a fluster. When their turn was over, they protested laughingly but made way for the next pair. Angelia repeated her routine, mimicking the steps in front of the couple so that they could follow her lead. When they had trouble keeping up, she took a moment and then switched places with the woman, showing her husband how to lead and how to maneuver the turns.

She was so caught up in the lesson that she had no idea Nicholas had joined them until she caught sight of him in the mirror. He was still dressed in his work clothes, a sleek black suit with a red-and-gray silk tie that was just beginning to loosen around his collar. For a brief second their eyes caught in the mirror, and then she had to turn, keeping up with the music.

Nicholas smiled at the other couples and then leaned against the wall, propping one leg up behind him and crossing his arms in front of his chest. He felt restless, not uncomfortable or embarrassed as he would have expected, but restless. The other couples were having a good time. They were laughing and tapping their feet and enjoying each stumble as much as each smoothly executed step. He envied their ease, their enjoyment, but most of all he envied the way the men got to hold Angelia in their arms, something he was constantly trying to deny himself.

He was getting tired of fighting, and watching her now in a red silk dress with her long black hair swirling around her shoulders, he realized that the battle was just about over and he was losing . . . or maybe he was winning. He wouldn't know until he let her into his life. It was a risk, not even a calculated one. Because how could you estimate someone as unpredictable and lovely as Angelia? He could get hurt...badly hurt.

He altered his position, his eyes never leaving her graceful, flowing figure. She was poetry in motion and, like the dance, she was sexy and seductive and complicated. What if he made a mistake? What if she rejected him?

Too much conjecture and not enough facts. That's why he was hesitating. He didn't like to make a move when he wasn't in control, when he didn't know what the outcome would be. But she was making him forget all that. He just wanted to wrap his arms around that tiny waist, hold her firmly in place against his body, make her feel what she did to him every time she smiled, every time she looked at him. He wanted to be part of her crazy, whirlwind life. He wanted to share her enthusiasm, her innocence, her optimism. Most of all, he just wanted to hold her.

The music stopped as she changed cassettes, and then she looked expectantly at the group.

"Now that we've mastered the basic steps, I want to put it together. But I'd like to show you the next move before we do it." She looked expectantly around the room. "Can I have a volunteer?"

"Why don't you use me?" Nicholas suggested.

She stared at him in amazement, remaining silent as he walked over to join her. "Nicholas," she whispered under her breath. His expression was serious but determined. "Are you sure?"

"Yes. I'd like to dance with you. Unless you'd rather not?"

"Are you kidding? Let's show them what you can do."

Nicholas took a deep breath as the group waited expectantly. He felt as nervous as a six-year-old at his first school play. "First you better show me."

"Don't worry. I won't let you down," she whispered. She walked over and punched the stereo button and then opened her arms to him.

He walked over, and with a hesitant step they began to dance. She ran through the first simple steps she had shown him before, and slowly he gained confidence. Then she began to move faster, encouraging him with discreet pressure on his arms or shoulder until he found his own rhythm. When the first combination ended and she broke away, he felt frustrated instead of relieved. He wanted to keep dancing with her. Watching her walk out of his arms was killing him.

Taking a deep breath, he stepped aside as she walked over to the other couples. He didn't want to think about the intensity of his feelings. They were too strong, too overwhelming. Lord, he had actually danced in front of a group of strangers, his guests. What had she done to him?

"Now, let's see the rest of you try it," Angelia said loudly, pushing the shakiness out of her voice. She turned on the music as the other couples moved into position. "Just do the first combination and then let yourself flow into the second, more difficult one. Nick and I will lead you." She turned around, looking for Nick, but he had vanished. She took a deep breath and forced a smile. "I guess I'll do this on my own. Let's begin."

She was just turning off the lights about an hour later when Nicholas reappeared in the hallway outside of the ballroom. His expression was a mixture of wariness and guilt.

"Hi," he said.

"You're back. I can't say I'm surprised. You seem to disappear and reappear at will. I thought you were enjoying yourself earlier, that we were making some progress." She folded her arms across her chest and waited.

"Isn't it enough that I got out there in front of all those people and actually danced?"

"I'm not sure. Is it enough for you?"

"You don't understand."

"Apparently not. But at the moment I'm too tired to try and figure you out."

"Can I offer you a cup of coffee?"

She wavered, thinking of her lonely little apartment. "Maybe a decaf. I don't want to be up all night."

"We can go up to my suite."

"I didn't realize you had a suite as well as an office here."

"Sometimes I stay the night if I'm working late."

He led her to the elevator and punched the button for the top floor, then turned a special key that allowed them access to his private suite of rooms.

Angelia gave a quick glance around the living room as she walked in. It had the usual attributes of luxury that she had come to relate with Nicholas, but once again very little in the way of warmth or personality.

While he started the hot water, she sank down on the sofa and leafed idly through a magazine lying on the coffee table. It was a business magazine, and most of the articles were on management styles or trends in economic growth. As she got more involved in the running of her school, she was also getting interested in becoming an effective manager and owner. While the art was important to her, she was beginning to think making a profit wouldn't be so bad, either. Then they could put on more lavish productions and recitals, really make their program special.

"Find anything interesting?" Nicholas asked, setting her coffee down on the table.

"More than you would think," she retorted, ignoring his amused glance. "At least I keep my mind open."

"So do I. If you have a copy of *Dance Review* or whatever, I'd be happy to take a look at it."

She sent him a disbelieving glance and then pulled her legs up underneath her on the couch as she looked around the room. "So this is where you come to relax. Where's the TV?"

"In the cabinet. Do you want to watch something?"

"Not really."

"Then maybe you'd like to join me in something that I find very relaxing or stimulating, depending on my partner."

"Should I ask you what it is, or just grab my purse and head for the door?"

He laughed. "It's nothing to be afraid of." Getting up, he walked over to one of the closets and pulled out a box.

"Monopoly?" she asked.

"Don't you like games?"

"Sure. But I don't think I've played one in about ten years."

"Want to give it a run with me? I think you can find out a great deal about a person by the way they play Monopoly. Martin, for instance, always wants the name property, you know, Park Place, things like that. Me, I like the railroads."

"So you can get out of town fast."

"Very funny. You'll be sorry you said that when you want me to bail you out of jail." He set up the board on the coffee table, counting out the money and laying out two playing pieces.

Angelia smiled, feeling suddenly rejuvenated, matching wits with Nick. And he didn't know that she had once been the Monopoly champion of Danforth Junior High.

Twenty minutes later she knew she had met her match. "I can't believe how many hotels you already own," she complained as Nick proudly added another hotel box to his collection. "Don't you ever take a breather?"

"That's the way you play the game."

"I've never met anyone as ruthless as you. I thought this was going to be a fun game."

"I'm having fun."

"That's because you've just about driven me bankrupt."

"You can always ask me for a loan. I'm a nice guy."

"I'd have better chances with a shark." She rolled the dice and clapped her hands as she landed on the only empty property on the board. "That's mine. Now you're blocked. And my rents are going up."

"That wasn't nice, Angelia."

"Nice guys finish last," she retorted. "I think you're rubbing off on me. Now things are going to go my way."

"Most women would have thrown the game by now," he said dryly. "Don't you know anything about the male ego?"

"I like to compete. Besides, the fun is in the playing, not the winning. If I didn't give you a game, you'd be bored stiff."

"But I'd still have my pride."

"Who cares about that?"

He shook his head at her honest statement. "You, Angelia, are one of a kind."

"No kidding. And you just landed on my skyscraper. That will be one hundred thousand dollars, please." Laughing, she accepted his money with a ready smile. "You're right, Nick. This is fun, maybe even better than dancing." She paused. "But then you'll probably never be able to compare the two."

"Probably not," he agreed. "Which reminds me. I'm going to be tied up the next couple of days. I'll try to fit in a lesson, but I'm not sure."

She sent him a steady, knowing look. "Whatever you want, Nick. But sooner or later you're going to have to face facts."

"I know. But right now the only fact I want to deal with is how I'm going to get back my railroad." He rolled the dice and groaned. "Go to jail. Damn. I hate to sit on that square doing nothing."

"Well, I do have a get-out-of-jail card, and I might be willing to give it to you ... for a price."

"How much?"

"I'm not talking money, Nick."

He stared into her wickedly dark eyes and felt his stomach jump into his throat. "I'd prefer to pay you in cash."

"I know you would. But that's not the deal. I want a kiss. One tiny little kiss. It's your call."

He sighed. "If I have to..." Then he leaned over the board and kissed her on the cheek.

She looked at him in disappointment. "That wasn't much of an effort."

"You want more?" he teased, sending her a broad grin. With an abrupt jerk he picked up the Monopoly board and threw it on the floor, scattering pieces and money in all directions. Then he gathered Angelia in his arms, pushing her back against the sofa until he was practically lying on top of her.

Laughing, she tried to push him away, but when his mouth touched hers, the laughter died between them. He raised his head, giving her a questioning look, and then he kissed her again, a long, soul-searching kiss that made her realize she wasn't just losing a game of Monopoly; she was losing her heart.

Chapter Eleven

"Nervous?" Nicholas asked casually as they walked through the terminal at Los Angeles International Airport five days later.

"Not really," Angelia replied. "I like to fly. The feeling of soaring into the clouds is great."

"What about the thought of crashing to the ground?"

"I don't think about it. But I'm sure you'll be worrying enough for both of us."

"Not on my own plane. I handpick my pilots, so I know exactly what level of experience I'm dealing with."

"I didn't realize we were going on a private plane."

"Company jet," he replied. "We bought one a few years ago when we began developing resorts outside of the U.S. In the long run it's been very cost-effective for us."

"What other resorts do you own?" she asked curiously.

"We own ten hotels across the United States of varying sizes. We have a resort in Australia, one in Hawaii and another in the Caribbean."

"Really? I had no idea your company was so large. No wonder you have so much money."

He laughed at her bluntness. "I had some help along the way. Martin's parents are very wealthy and helped me with the initial investments. They still own a healthy share of the company, and there are a few other private investors, as well."

"But you still run things, don't you?"

"That's what it says in my job description. But Martin actually does quite a bit. He may act like a carefree guy, but he's very sharp when it comes to business."

"And a good friend, too," she added, remembering their brief conversation.

Nicholas sent her a wary look. "What did he tell you?"

"Nothing too personal."

"For some reason that doesn't make me feel much better. Martin's idea of privacy is not the same as mine."

"Good morning, Mr. Hunter." A smiling woman in uniform greeted them as they reached the end of the terminal walkway. "You're all ready to board."

"Thank you, Jessica."

"Have a good flight."

"We hope so." He put a hand on the small of Angelia's back and ushered her through the door and up the steps to the aircraft.

They were met inside by another smiling woman whose badge identified her only as Carol. After exchanging greetings, she went back into the galley area while Nicholas led Angelia into the main cabin. There were no standard airline seats, but instead comfortable reclining chairs and sofas. Angelia felt more like she was being seated in someone's living room than in an airplane.

"This is incredible," she murmured, sending a disbelieving smile over to Nicholas.

"It works."

She rolled her eyes and took a seat in one of the chairs, adjusting her skirt beneath her. "How did you ever get used to all this? It would be different if you had been born into money. But what extremes you've seen in your life."

"It took a long time to feel right. Although sometimes I do still have to pinch myself." He settled back in a chair, taking off his suit coat and loosening his tie. "It's going to be a long flight, so make yourself comfortable."

"I don't think that will be hard." She let out a small sigh and glanced out the window as the engines began to hum. In truth she was feeling a little nervous, but it wasn't about flying. It was about Nick.

Since their Monopoly game on Monday night, he had been deliberately absent, avoiding her calls and her attempts to schedule another lesson. If it hadn't been for the efficient messages from his secretary, she would have thought the entire trip was off. But he had shown up promptly at seven o'clock in the morning, and with a casual smile hauled her bags into his car before proceeding to the airport.

He hadn't mentioned the tango or the heart-stopping kiss that had ended their game, and she had been too confused to say much of anything herself. The week's absence had only made her feelings grow stronger, and seeing him again made her realize how much she had missed him and how much she was going to miss him when this was all over.

"Now you do look nervous," Nick proclaimed, reading her thoughtful expression with concern. "Something wrong?"

She shook her head. "No, just thinking about everything."

"Bad week?"

"The usual. What about you?"

"A lot of last-minute details to take care of."

"Oh. I thought maybe you were avoiding me."

"Why would I do that?"

"You tell me."

"Maybe a little," he conceded. "I had to clear my desk for this trip...and I thought we needed some breathing space."

She looked at him in surprise. "Why?"

He shrugged. "Things have been moving pretty fast, and I needed to take a step back."

"From the tango...or me?" she asked daringly.

"Both."

"Oh." It was the only response she could think of after such a blunt statement, followed by the closing shutters in his eyes. She might be getting under his skin, but he was damned if he was going to tell her. She shook her head in frustration.

"Right now I just want to get through this trip. The next few days are going to be a trial for both of us. Have you thought about contacting your father?"

She sighed, allowing him to change the subject only because she really didn't know what she wanted to say to him yet. "I've thought and thought, but I still haven't made a decision. Maybe when I get there, things will seem more clear to me. Have you ever wanted to find your mother?"

"No," he said abruptly. "Not in a long time."

"No unanswered questions?"

"Not really. I don't know exactly why she gave me up, but I have a good idea. And what's the point of dredging up the past now? I am what I am."

"Maybe she had a good reason for leaving. Maybe she did it because she loved you."

"Maybe she did. But that doesn't really make it any more palatable. It might have been easier if I had been a baby when she left. But I was four years old. I still remember her. I remember things that we did together, the lies that she told me about always being there for me."

"I know," she said sincerely. "I feel that way about my father. We're two of a kind."

"Except that I've come to terms with my past. And you still aren't sure." He paused. "We'll be spending tonight and tomorrow in Buenos Aires and then we'll fly down to Juan Carlos's home on Sunday. If your father is in Buenos Aires or in Necochea, you should be able to reach him."

She took a deep breath and let it out slowly. "Thanks for not offering me any advice. I know I need to make this decision on my own. I just feel that somehow I need to resolve things before I can move forward."

"Sometimes you don't have a choice. You just have to go on even without the answers. Forget the past."

"I don't know if you can ever entirely let go of the past. It's a part of who you are. It's what makes you keep going."

"Maybe," he conceded, thinking of the magazine picture that had driven him for so long. That elusive search for paradise. The feeling that he had really made it. Those goals weren't as clear as they had once been. Not since Angelia had danced into his life, upsetting all of his carefully prepared goals with her spontaneity and zest for life. Even now, watching her prepare for the flight with her own special enthusiasm, he felt his weariness lifting, his eagerness rekindling. She had so much to give him, but what could he give her in return?

"Now you're the one looking somber," she said lightly, interrupting his thoughts. "Worried about our pilot's capabilities?"

He smiled. "No. I think your optimism is contagious."

"Good. Now, when do we eat?"

He laughed. "Whenever you like. We can have breakfast once we take off, then lunch, then dinner."

"It is going to be a long flight, isn't it?"

"I'm afraid so. And we will have to stop in Mexico City for a short time. But we have several movies on board and plenty of reading material. There's also a bed on the other side of that curtain. If you get tired, you can just take a nap. We won't be getting in to Buenos Aires until late tonight."

"Sounds like you've thought of everything. I don't think I've ever met anyone who plans as much as you do."

"It's just the way I am. I can't seem to stop organizing things."

"Don't apologize. It's not bad. We're just different. And that's not bad, either."

"I can think of worse things," he admitted as the plane began to taxi toward the runway.

As the engines roared, she reached out her hand to hold his. He looked down at her fingers suddenly entwined with his in bemusement. "I thought you liked to fly."

"I do. But I must admit takeoffs are a little unnerving."

Her smile was innocent, but her eyes were twinkling. And suddenly he was grinning back. He didn't care if she was terrified or simply using a ready excuse. He liked holding her hand. In fact he might just hang on to it for the rest of the flight.

By the time they arrived at their hotel in Buenos Aires, Angelia was exhausted. As Nick had predicted, the flight had been long even with all the comforts of home. At the moment all she could think of was a warm, soft bed and eight hours of oblivion.

The bellboy escorted them to a large suite on the upper floor of the hotel, complete with two bedrooms, a living room and even a bar area. More luxury, she thought with a weary smile. "This is nice."

"Yes," he agreed, taking a look around. "Almost makes me wish I had my own hotel here."

"Why don't you?"

"Money, location and about a hundred other reasons. In the last three years I've been concentrating more on getting out of the big cities and getting into the more picturesque areas." He paused, studying her face with concern. "You look tired. Take whatever room you like. Unless you're hungry?"

"No," she groaned, thinking of all the food they had consumed on the flight. "I'm stuffed."

He smiled at her and instinctively reached out to tuck a strand of hair behind her ear. Their eyes caught, and suddenly she wasn't tired anymore but vibrantly alive. They were alone together in a hotel room, just the two of them and their crazy desire.

His fingers slid down to stroke her cheek, and his blue eyes darkened as he watched her changing expression. "You better go to bed," he muttered, but still he didn't move. His fingers gently caressed her face, drifting down to the full generous outline of her mouth.

She parted her lips, landing a gentle kiss on his roaming fingers, and he let out a long, deep breath.

"Kiss me good-night," she invited, knowing it was dangerous, but she didn't care. She just wanted to taste him again, to feel his arms around her.

He hesitated and then, cupping her face with both hands, he lowered his head. His kiss started out gentle and then deepened in intensity as she welcomed his tongue into her mouth. Her hands came to rest on his waist, her fingers tightening on his belt buckle as she pulled him closer to her, hoping that the kiss would go on forever, knowing that it shouldn't, that there were too many barriers still between them.

"You are so tempting," he breathed, his mouth coming to rest against her cheek.

"So are you," she murmured. "This is crazy, though."

"Isn't it? But I've been wanting to do this all day."

"Why didn't you?"

"I didn't want you to think I was taking advantage of the situation."

"Always so cautious."

"For both our sakes."

She smiled. "Maybe. But I know I can trust you."

"We should probably call it a night."

"Probably," she agreed, but neither one moved.

"If you don't go into your room right now, I may not let you go at all."

Her heart raced at his husky words, but even as she smiled, she knew they were a bluff. And as she pulled back, she smiled up at him. "Maybe I don't want to go."

"Angelia," he said warningly. "This isn't the time to play games."

"I already told you. I don't play games. And I don't like to hide my feelings. Someday we're going to talk about what's going on between us, Nick. Not tonight, but soon."

He nodded his head, his jaw tightening. "Just go to bed, Angelia."

She hesitated and then turned to pick up her suitcase. A few minutes later she walked into her room and shut the door behind her.

When she was gone, Nicholas let out a long, ragged breath and then walked over to the bar. Reaching for a bottle of brandy, he poured himself a drink and then moved to the window and stared out at the lights of Buenos Aires. Things had been hot enough in California. What were they going to be like here, where the nights were sultry and warm, where he felt reckless and tempted?

He tossed the brandy down his throat and walked into his bedroom, shutting the door quietly but firmly behind him.

* * *

"It's hard to believe I'm back in Buenos Aires," Angelia said quietly as she and Nicholas stepped out of their hotel after breakfast the next morning. She took a long, deep breath of fresh air and smiled with enthusiasm at the sunny blue sky over their heads.

It was summertime in Argentina, and the morning temperature was already reaching into the eighties. She slipped her sweater off and tied it loosely around the waist of her short-sleeved sundress. "I want to see everything, Casa Rosada, the cathedral, the Plaza de Mayo."

"Slow down. We only have one day here. I'd have scheduled in more time if I'd known you were going to be this excited about being back in your homeland."

"I was a fool to even think twice about coming." She sent him a bright smile. "You've given me the opportunity of a lifetime. I can't thank you enough."

"Don't thank me yet. We still have a few things to get through."

"I don't want to think about any of that right now. Can we go for a walk?" She paused. "Or do you have some business to take care of?"

"I do have some paperwork upstairs," he said slowly. "But it can probably wait for a few hours."

"Then spend the day with me," she said impulsively. "Let's just pretend we're here on holiday."

"I'm beginning to think that every day with you is a holiday. You have a way of turning all my carefully thought out plans upside down."

"A little shake-up is good for you."

"Let me check in with the front desk. I tentatively reserved a driver for us today."

"But I don't want to see Buenos Aires from the back seat of a car. I want to get out and walk, soak up the atmosphere."

Nick sighed, but she caught a glimpse of a lurking smile in his eyes.

"What do you say?" she prodded. "Are you with me?"

"I'm in." He threw an arm around her shoulders. "Let's go."

Their hotel was located on Calle Florida, a street filled with hotels and shops, and as they walked along, Angelia looked in delight from one side of the street to the other. The city had changed a great deal in the past eighteen years, but she felt the familiar memories assail her as they passed by restaurants where she had shared meals with her father and his parents, her cousins, the family that had once been her own.

At times she felt her enthusiasm slipping into melancholy, but she forced it aside. This was her homeland, and in many ways she felt an affinity to the city that was a spectrum of influences from European to Italian to French and Spanish, just as she was a mixture of cultures.

For three hours they walked, stopping when they felt like it, sharing their own thoughts on the city. She found Nicholas to be an informed guide, having learned a great deal about the city and the country on his recent trips. She in turn related the old tales of lore that she remembered from her childhood. By the time the afternoon sun was beginning to set, her feet were tired and her stomach was rumbling.

Calling a halt to their tour, she stopped in front of a *confiteria,* an Argentine version of a tearoom. "Are you ready for a break?"

Nicholas rolled his eyes. "About two hours ago."

"Why don't we get a drink, maybe a sandwich?"

"Good idea. We won't be eating dinner for hours. That's one thing that I've never gotten used to in this country. They eat lunch around five and dinner around nine or ten. In fact the streets come alive after midnight."

"Maybe that's why I'm a night person. It must be in my blood."

As they walked inside, a waitress led them over to a table by the window, and overlooking the crowded street, they ordered a glass of wine and an open-faced grilled-beef sandwich.

"What do you think of your hometown now?" Nicholas asked curiously.

"It's beautiful." She sighed. "But..."

"What?"

"It's different than I remembered. Not as quaint or as warm as in my memories. I can't believe there are actually pizza places and hamburger joints."

"Progress. Time moves on."

"Too fast, sometimes."

"Or too slow," he replied. "Maybe you should have come back sooner. You would have seen a more gradual change. It would have been easier to adjust."

"I don't think I was ready to come back before. And I'm not really disappointed. I know that this city is just moving along with the rest of the world. But it is a little sad not to see the open markets where my grandmother used to bargain. She was a wealthy woman, but she would haggle with the best of them."

"Are your grandparents still alive?"

"My grandfather died before we left. And my grandmother died about ten years ago. She used to write to me. Never to my mother. That's why I couldn't write back. I would have felt guilty, as if I were betraying her. Now I wish I had." She paused, deciding it was time to change the subject. "What about your grandparents?"

"According to the nuns, I didn't have any."

"They died before you were born?"

"Apparently so."

"So your mother was all alone."

"That's what they said."

"And then you were all alone."

He took a long sip of his drink and then shook his head. "I know what you're trying to say. Now that I'm older, I understand the mess she got herself into and I've tried to forgive her. But it's difficult to forget. As for my being alone, I got used to it. Now I prefer it. At least, I did up until a few weeks ago."

Her breath caught at the sudden look in his eyes. "I feel the same way."

"You? You've never been alone. You're friendly and gregarious. You have hundreds of friends and a family that loves you."

"But I've still been lonely. My mother and I have never really been close. We care a lot, but we don't totally understand each other. And Michael was a lot younger than me, plus the fact that he had a different father and he couldn't really relate to my past. It's been difficult to share my feelings with any-one...until now. In some ways I feel like we're soul mates."

Nicholas stared back at her, but he didn't say any-thing. Then the waitress brought their food over, and in the midst of eating and drinking, their intimate conversation was tabled. The sun was fading over the horizon when they finished, and by the time they walked back out to the street it was nearly dark.

"It's getting late," Nicholas said idly, looking around for a taxi.

"What time is Martin coming in tonight?"

"After eleven. He would have come with us, but he had to go to New York on the way."

"The two of you jet around the world as often as I go to the deli," she remarked with a laugh. "And you make it sound so easy."

"It's really not as glamorous as it sounds. The trips are usually filled with meetings and appointments, and a lot of heavy lunches and dull conversations."

"Not like this trip," she teased.

He smiled back. "No, this trip does not compare. And I have to admit this city is one of my favorites, especially in the evening, when the music begins to play and dark-eyed, beautiful women seem to be everywhere."

She smiled at the whimsy in his statement. "Feeling a little romance in your soul?"

"Never. But when the sun goes down, I don't think I can be held accountable for my actions. In fact I'm having a little trouble remembering why we're here. I'm tempted to forget the meeting and my business and just spend some time with you exploring this town, getting better acquainted, finding out if we really are soul mates."

His voice turned husky, and she stared at him, entranced by the look in his eyes as well as his words. "That's a dangerous idea. And you don't like to live dangerously."

"Maybe I'm changing."

Chapter Twelve

A middle-aged, dark-haired woman sat behind a large, imposing desk. She looked up in surprise at Angelia's sudden appearance. "May I help you?" she asked in Spanish, changing to English when Angelia didn't respond.

"Yes," Angelia said finally, having understood the question in both languages but still being assailed by doubts. "I'd like to see Señor Roberto Martinez."

"Do you have an appointment?"

"No." She paused, taking another deep breath. "I'm his daughter, Angelia."

The secretary let out a small gasp. "You're little Angelia?"

"Yes. May I see him, please?"

"He's not here. He's already left for the day. If you had called . . ."

Her heart sank at the words. "He's gone."

"Yes. I'm sorry."

"That's all right. It's probably better this way." She turned to leave.

"Would you like to leave a message? Can he get in touch with you somewhere?"

Angelia hesitated and then shook her head. "I don't think so. I'm leaving in the morning."

"I know he'll be sorry he missed you."

The woman sounded sincere. In fact she looked almost upset by the fact that her father wasn't there to see her. Was it possible that he still thought of her? That he still cared? Angelia turned to leave.

"Wait. If you really want to see him, he'll be at the El Teron Nightclub tonight after ten o'clock."

Angelia paused at the door and then walked out, making a mental note of the information. Her mind was racing with questions as she traveled down the elevator to the lobby, mentally debating whether she should pursue her father any farther.

Nicholas took one look at her troubled face and opened his arms. She stepped into them without thinking, resting her cheek against the comforting warmth of his shoulder. His arms tightened around her, but he didn't say anything.

After a moment she pulled away. "Thanks."

"No problem." He searched her face for some sign of how to continue. "What happened?"

"He wasn't there."

Nicholas let out a long breath. "I'm sorry."

"I don't know if you should be. Maybe it's better this way."

"What now?"

"I'm not sure. His secretary seemed to recognize my name as if he'd talked about me. She told me that he would be at the El Teron Nightclub later tonight."

His answering look was long and pointed.

"Yes, I'm going," she said finally. "I've come this far. I might as well go the rest of the way."

"I hope I haven't pressured you into this. In fact maybe you should back off right now. You made the effort, and you came up empty."

"That's true. But I don't know if I could live with myself if I didn't make one last try, especially since she gave me the information."

"Whatever you want," Nicholas replied as they walked out of the building.

"I guess I have a few hours to think about it. Do you want to go back to the hotel now? Maybe think about rehearsing the tango? We have a dance tomorrow night, Nick. You and me in front of a whole roomful of people. I don't want to let you down."

"If anything, it will be the other way around," Nicholas said grimly, calling for a taxi.

She let the comment pass until they were in the taxi and on their way back to the hotel, but when he showed no signs of resuming the conversation, she pushed ahead.

"What is it about this dance that bothers you so much?" she asked in frustration. "Is it me? Do you hate the thought of holding me in your arms, of having to trust me for just a few minutes?"

"No," he said forcefully, shaking his head at the same time. "It's much more complicated than that."

"Then tell me what it is. Make me understand. Maybe I can help."

He sighed, thinking about her words. "When I was a teenager, I went to a dance at the public high school. I asked the prettiest girl in the room to dance because the Sisters at the convent had taught me what they

thought were the right steps." He made a sour face at
the memory. "It was horrible. I fumbled and stumbled and stepped on her feet. And then the worst happened, she walked away from me in the middle of the
dance floor. And the other kids laughed because I
didn't know how to dance. I didn't know how to have
fun. I was humiliated."

"I'm sorry," she said quietly, reaching out a hand
to touch his shoulder. "Kids can be very cruel."

"It sounds stupid to even remember such an inci-
dent now," he said roughly. "But that dance just
symbolized everything about my life that I hated. I
was always the different kid, the one that didn't fit in.
Over the years I learned how to talk and how to dress
and basically how to be the kind of man I wanted to
be. But I never did learn to dance. And I guess this
tango business is a reminder of everything that I
thought I had left behind. I almost feel that if I fail at
this, then everything that I have done is just nothing."

Angelia stared at him in concern, wanting to say the
right things but not sure how to go about it.

"But I have to do it," he continued. "Because I
want that land more than anything." He reached into
his pocket for his wallet and then pulled out a faded
magazine photograph and handed it to her.

"What's this?" she asked curiously.

"Paradise." He paused, studying the picture. "I cut
this out when I was eleven years old. At the time I was
still living in the convent orphanage. All I had that was
mine was a cot to sleep on, a blanket and about three
sets of clothes. I used to dream about living in a place
like this. Some people would say that over the years I
became obsessed with it. All my goals have been di-

rected toward acquiring a piece of property that looks like this, and the land that Juan Carlos owns is perfect.''

She stared at the yellowing, faded picture and felt her heart turn over at his confidence. In her mind she could see him as a little boy, lonely and unloved, searching for something better. But did he really think a piece of land could make him completely happy? Somehow she didn't think so. He needed more than that. He needed love. He needed her.

"So that's why I have to do this." He took the photograph out of her hand and stuffed it back into his wallet.

"I think I understand," she said finally. "And I believe I can help you get what you want." She paused deliberately. "You trusted me enough to share this with me. Will you trust me enough not to let you down tomorrow night? Will you dance the tango with me?''

"I don't have any other choice," he said.

"But you do. You just have to figure out what it is," she murmured, settling back in her seat as the taxi pulled up in front of their hotel.

A series of messages from his company were waiting for Nicholas when they arrived, and while he caught up on paperwork, Angelia took a shower and dressed for dinner. There was no time for further conversation or even a brief rehearsal of the tango before their reservations at eight o'clock that night.

Angelia opted for dinner at a local restaurant, but although the food was delicious and the atmosphere pleasant, her mind was still wrestling with the problem of whether or not to confront her father. She was also worried about Nicholas and how she could help him get through the tango the next evening.

He in turn did little to push the conversation along, and was so withdrawn that she wondered if he regretted his earlier confidence.

They finished their meal just before ten, early by Argentine standards, and as they walked out of the restaurant, Nicholas turned to her with an inquiring expression. "What do you want to do now?"

"I knew you were going to ask me that," she replied as a taxi pulled up in front of them almost on cue.

Nicholas ushered her into the seat, and when the driver turned for instructions, Angelia leaned forward. "El Teron Nightclub," she said firmly.

The driver nodded and started the car. Angelia turned to Nicholas, and he took her hand in a reassuring grip. They arrived at the club within minutes, and once inside the dimly lit interior, Angelia hesitated. How on earth was she going to find her father in this crowded room? The image in her mind was eighteen years old. He probably looked completely different now.

"I don't know what to do," she said with a hint of panic in her voice.

"Let me ask the hostess if your father had a reservation," Nicholas said easily, stepping past her to talk with one of the women behind the front counter. After a brief conversation he returned.

"What did she say?"

"She said to take a seat down toward the front, and we won't be able to miss him," Nicholas replied. "That's all she would say."

"Well, let's go."

She followed Nicholas through the smoky room to a table tucked away in the corner. They settled down and ordered some wine and then watched the crowd idly as the band swung into another number. The song was lush and romantic, and Angelia felt a tightening in her gut at the sultry words of love. That's what this was all about. Her love. Not just for her father, but for Nicholas. The realization hit her like a rush of cold water. That's what had been bothering her all evening.

She loved Nicholas. Looking across the table at his handsome profile, she felt her heart turn over. He wasn't the kind of man she would have thought to fall in love with. He was sensible and logical to a fault, cautious and predictable. But he was also caring and sensitive, tender and strong. And her heart ached at the things he had told her. More than anything, she wanted to bring joy into his life. She wanted to show him what love and family were all about.

The doubts she had about her own family suddenly seemed unimportant in comparison. She had lacked a father, but her mother had always been there for her, and her brother was dearer to her than anyone in the world. That was two people that loved her, two more than Nicholas had.

"Do you see him?" he asked, breaking in on her rampaging thoughts.

She shook her head belatedly, suddenly realizing that finding her father wasn't really that important anymore. It wouldn't change the way she felt about Nicholas. She already trusted him. She had already given her heart. The future was in her own hands, not in her father's.

"Are you all right?" Nicholas asked with concern.

She took a deep breath, still bemused by her own thoughts. "I'm okay." She turned her head, taking a quick look around the room, but it was dark and smoky and the faces she saw were a blur.

"Maybe we should walk around," Nicholas suggested.

"No. Let's just have our drinks and enjoy the music." She smiled as the familiar strains of the tango began. "This must be our night."

Nicholas groaned, recognizing the haunting music from his dreams. "What did I do to deserve this?"

"Shh. The dancers are coming out. Maybe you can pick up a few tips."

The spotlight swirled around the room, finally settling on the couple in the center of the dance floor as they began to dance the tango. Their movements were stylish and in perfect harmony, Angelia thought, marveling at their expertise. It wasn't until they circled the room and she caught a glimpse of the man's face that she let out a small gasp.

He was older now. His hair was gray and his body was more filled out. But there was no mistaking his identity. The man dancing the tango was her father.

"Angelia?" Nick questioned sharply.

She didn't reply, because at that moment the dancers parted and moved toward the crowd, laughingly calling for partners.

"Are you okay? You're white as a sheet. Let's get out of here."

She shook her head as her father circled the room toward their table. Making a sudden decision, she stood up, catching her father's eye. He moved swiftly over to her, taking her hand and pulling her onto the dance floor. The crowd cheered as he placed a red rose behind her ear, and then they began to dance.

He moved better than anyone she had ever danced with, his movements sure and confident. And it wasn't until he swung her into the middle of the spotlight that he really looked into her face. And then he faltered, staring at her with eyes as brown as her own.

"Angelia," he whispered, coming to a halt in the center of the room.

"Yes."

For a long moment they stared at each other, and then the crowd began calling out, encouraging them to dance. Angelia started the movements herself, forcing him to finish the dance. And when the music ended, he bowed and she walked back to her table.

Nicholas stood up as she approached, helping her into her chair with a concerned look. "What was that all about?"

"That man is my father."

"Yes, I am."

Nicholas got to his feet again, exchanging a pointed look with the older man now standing at their table. "Why don't you join us," he suggested, sending a questioning look in Angelia's direction. "Unless..."

"It's okay," she said flatly.

"I'll leave you two alone."

"No, please stay." Angelia looked at him pleadingly, and without another word he pulled up a chair for her father and they sat down.

"I don't know what to say," Roberto Martinez said haltingly. "You're here, after all these years. And so beautiful." His hand reached out to stroke her hair, but as she flinched, he dropped it awkwardly into his lap. "You must hate me."

"I don't know how I feel anymore," she said honestly.

"I've thought about you for so long, wondered how you were, if you would ever come back here."

"I'm here on business."

"Then this was a coincidence?"

"Not entirely. I stopped by your office this afternoon. Your secretary told me you would be here tonight. I just took a chance."

"I'm so glad you did. I can't believe you're all grown-up now. You look just like your grandmother. I wish she could see you now."

"So do I. But more than that, I wish I could have known her for a longer time."

He nodded sadly. "I'm so sorry."

She looked around the shadowy room, but no one was paying them any attention, and after a moment she voiced the question that had been burning in her heart for so many years.

"Why didn't you call me?"

"I knew you would ask me that one day." He paused. "In the beginning I couldn't call. And later I thought it was better for you and your mother if I just stayed out of your life."

"What happened between you? I thought you were so much in love," Angelia muttered.

"She didn't tell you?"

"Not a word for all these years."

He sighed. "It's a long story and not a very nice one."

"That's what my mother always says."

"I did love her and you, but I unfortunately also loved alcohol. I had some business problems when you were about five. That's when the trouble really began. I started to drink to relax. But it didn't help. And every time I looked into your mother's beautiful face, I felt guilty and ashamed that I was failing her. So I drank more. And when I drank, my temper would get hot. I would say terrible things to Michelle, accuse her of flirting with other men. Looking back, I realize how lonely she must have been, but at the time I couldn't see past the whiskey in my glass.''

He closed his eyes painfully, finally opening them. "And then one night, the unthinkable happened. We were arguing, and I hit her. I couldn't stop myself. Michelle left that night. I tried to rationalize my behavior, put all the blame on her, and for days I just buried myself in alcohol and parties, lying about where you and your mother were. I sank lower and lower until everyone finally began to see the truth. It took me another six years to get myself out of the hole I had fallen into. I'd take a step forward and then fall back. My mother urged me to go after you and Michelle, but I had a lot of pride, and I had lost so much by then I didn't think I had anything to offer.'' He paused. "I didn't want to hurt you anymore, and I knew your mother would never forgive me for what I had done.''

Angelia stared at him somberly as he finished speaking. Everything was beginning to make sense, and instead of the anger she had thought she would feel, she felt only a hint of bitterness overshadowed by pity. In the candlelight of their table, she could see the signs of dissipation and the pain in his eyes. He had admitted to some terrible things, but he had suffered, too.

"Thank you for telling me,'' she said finally. "It helps to understand.''

"How is your mother?"

"She's fine."

"I'm glad. And you?"

She smiled for the first time, exchanging a warm look with Nicholas. "I'm getting better by the minute."

"I wish we had more time to talk. There are so many things I want to hear about, but unfortunately I have another performance in a few minutes."

"I'm glad you're still dancing the tango. I've never forgotten the image of you and Mom dancing together, the joy and love on your faces."

"Nor have I. And you dance just like her. Can we talk again? Please."

Angelia hesitated. "I'd like that, but let me call you. I need a little time."

"I understand. I'll say good night, then, but not goodbye." He shook hands with Nicholas before he left to go backstage.

"What do you think now?" Nicholas asked.

"I'm not sure. It's hard to take it all in. At least he was honest."

"He still loves you."

Her eyes misted for a moment. "It's hard to kill love off entirely. I don't know how I feel about him, but there is still a connection there that I can't turn my back on." She paused, taking a sip of her wine. "One thing I do know for sure is that you are really a terrific guy."

"Me? I'm just an innocent bystander here."

"You gave me the push I needed and a great deal of support."

He shrugged his shoulders and tried to brush off her compliment. "Do you want to stay and watch your father dance again?"

"No. I'd rather go somewhere else . . . with you."

"Angelia," he said warningly. "I don't think I like the look in your eyes."

"That's too bad. Because I intend to spend the next few hours looking only at you."

"I think I need another drink."

"Let's take a walk in the moonlight."

"The moonlight, huh?"

"Unless you want to volunteer to dance with the lady next time?"

"Let's walk. Maybe it will be cooler out there," he said, tugging at his tie.

"I doubt it," she replied with a laugh, preceding him out of the nightclub.

They walked for a few blocks in companionable silence. When a group of rowdy people bumped into Angelia, Nicholas put an arm around her, holding her close to his side. She rested her own arm around his waist, enjoying the warmth of their embrace, the joyful realization that she was in love with this man and that she was finally free to give in to that love.

Her happiness made her feel like dancing, and when they passed by an outdoor café brimming with music, she laughingly dragged him in behind her. The band was playing American music, and she pulled him into the center of the crowd as the Latin American version of Madonna filled the air.

"What do I do now?" Nicholas asked loudly.

"Just move your feet. No fancy steps here. Whoops." She laughed again as someone bumped into her from behind.

Nicholas stared at her in bemusement. The red rose was still in her dark hair, the vibrant colors contrasting with the pale white of her dress. When she smiled up at him, he felt his heart stop beating. She was the most beautiful thing he had seen, so alive. He wanted to share the laughter that sparkled from her lips, somehow capture the intense feeling of happiness that rumbled through him whenever she looked his way.

She reached out her hands to him and did a silly turn, landing against his chest, and he couldn't help smiling. She wasn't a sophisticated dancer now, just a woman having fun—with him. All too soon the crowd formed a snakelike line and pulled them apart.

He suddenly found his hands on the waist of another woman and someone else behind him. Angelia was caught up on the other side, and without her he felt suddenly lost, but the music continued and he surprised himself with the ease with which he fell into their crazy antics.

By the time the music stopped, he was breathless, and when Angelia suggested they continue their walk he readily agreed. The streets were quieter now as they moved farther away from the nightclub district, toward the residential area and a shadowy park.

At the entrance to the park was a fountain spurting a rainbow of colors against the dark night sky.

Angelia paused, and Nicholas stopped right behind her, pulling her against his chest.

"It's gorgeous," she whispered. "I don't think I've seen a prettier sight."

"Or maybe everything about this night is magic," he murmured in her ear.

She turned to face him. "I don't think it's magic. I think it's you."

"Not me."

"Then us. When we're together, something special happens."

"Because you're a witch," he replied with a smile.

"Because I'm a woman," she corrected. "And because you are an incredibly wonderful man." Her voice caught on the words. "Kiss me, Nick."

The words were barely out of her mouth when his lips descended on hers in a crushing kiss that sent a rush of desire down to the tips of her toes. His mouth told her everything that he couldn't say in words, how much he wanted her, how deep his feelings were.

His lips trailed across her face, dropping lightning-quick kisses on her cheeks, her earlobes and down to the base of her neck while his hands roamed freely up and down the length of her spine. She felt hot and then cold as a sudden breeze sent drops of water from the fountain right into their faces.

Gasping, they broke apart. Nicholas looked at the fountain and then at the moisture on her face. "Every time I kiss you, I get wet."

"Maybe you should pick your spots better," she teased, tucking her arm into his and resting her head against his shoulder. "I don't think I'll ever forget this night, Nick. And I know I won't ever be able to forget you." Her eyes turned serious as she looked at him.

"I don't want you to forget me."

"But you don't want a woman in your life," she reminded him, hoping he would disagree with her.

"Maybe I'm changing."

It was something, but it wasn't enough. She wanted him to be absolutely sure of his feelings for her. "Let's go back to the hotel. Martin should be getting in any time, and I'm sure you want to talk to him about to-morrow."

"Martin is the last person on my mind at the moment," he said roughly. "Although I wouldn't mind going back to the hotel for an entirely different reason."

"Not tonight, Nick. Not with so much riding on tomorrow. You have a chance of getting what you always wanted, your own slice of paradise. It's going to be a big day. I think we should call it a night. And it's not because I don't want to. It's because I want it to be perfect."

He hesitated and then shrugged. "You're right. You're being sensible, logical and matter-of-fact. And I wish to hell you weren't."

She smiled. "Good, we're making progress."

What he always wanted was suddenly convoluted, Nicholas decided the next day, as he walked along the stretch of land that would be the foundation for his resort. The sky overhead was still a royal blue, the sand white, the water clear and beckoning. It looked like his paradise, but it didn't feel quite right anymore.

There was something missing. Angelia.

She was waiting in the house for him to return from his lonely sojourn. She had wanted to come with him to see the property, but he had found excuses to be alone, because for some reason he didn't want her to see this yet. He didn't want her to look at his paradise and find it wanting.

But it was. His head was finally beginning to clear. He didn't need this strip of land to be happy. He didn't have to dance the tango for a group of strangers to seal this deal. Because it wasn't important anymore. His paradise wasn't a strip of land; it was Angelia's smile, her warm, loving personality, her gift of joy.

She had danced into his life and changed it completely. He would never be the same again, with or without her. He had been lying to himself, believing he could walk away from her at the end of the trip without any regrets. He already regretted the fact that he had let so much time go by without telling her how he felt.

But then she had never told him, either. The old insecurities flared within him. But this time he refused to bow under. He wasn't going to run and hide, to bury himself in his work because he was afraid to live. Everything in his life he had earned with single-minded determination, and he was damned if he would let the most important person in his life get away without a fight. He would show her how he felt in the only way she would truly understand... the tango.

"Where is Nicholas?" Angelia asked in desperation as Martin searched the room for his friend and partner.

"He should be here. I saw him about an hour ago, and everything seemed fine."

"I don't think so. He's been absentminded all day and very tense. What if he doesn't show up?"

Martin laid a hand on hers reassuringly. "It won't be your fault, Angelia. It's his business. If he wants to let it go because he's afraid..."

"He wouldn't have to be afraid if he would only trust me."

"There he is," Martin said with relief as Nicholas walked into the room.

Angelia let out a long sigh as he walked over to the table, exchanging hellos with Juan Carlos and some of his guests. She felt a little of her unease fade away as he made his way toward her. He looked fantastic tonight in a black tuxedo that was the picture of elegance. Even if he stumbled on the dance floor, he would still make a fine figure.

"I was worried about you," she said quietly when he joined them.

"I'm fine," he replied. "We're going to dance the tango first and then have dinner."

"Good. I don't think I'll be able to eat until we get this over with."

"Nervous?" he asked with a smile.

She looked at him in disbelief. "Yes. Aren't you?"

"Not anymore." He paused as Juan Carlos got to his feet. "This is it. Let's go."

He led her up to the front of the large dining room, which had been cleared for their performance. Several musicians waited as Juan Carlos announced their names, and then a hush fell over the group as the music began to play softly, gathering force as they took the floor.

"Just follow my lead," she whispered.

"No. You follow mine."

She looked at him in surprise as he took her hand with confidence, and they moved into their beginning combination. He was different tonight. She realized it immediately when he began to change the steps. Following in wonderment, she matched his moves with some of her own as his blue eyes invited her to play along.

The rest of the audience faded from her mind. It was just her and Nicholas on the dance floor. His steps might not have been definitive tango, but they were precise and sharp. She in turn added the flavor, the emotion, pulling him along in a passionate combination. Together they were unbeatable.

When the music reached its final crescendo, Nicholas captured her in his arms and swung her backward over his thigh in a traditional dip. For a split second her fingers tightened on his arms, and he looked deep into her eyes. Then he pulled her back up, and before she could speak, his mouth covered hers in a long passionate kiss that drew a round of applause from the crowd.

"Nicholas?" she murmured, ignoring the rest of the people in the room.

"I love you," he said, watching the beaming smile spread across her face.

"I love you, too."

"Hallelujah!" Martin called out, drawing a few laughs and another round of applause.

With a smile Nicholas turned to the group, still holding her tightly in his arms. "I'd like to thank you for this night. For the past couple of weeks I've been trying to find ways to get out of doing this tango. And today I finally realized that I did have a choice. I looked at your land, and it's still beautiful and valuable, but I can live without it. What I can't live without is this beautiful woman." He paused, smiling down at the wonderment on her face. "But I knew she would think I was only trying to get out of this dance again. And I wanted her to know that I would do anything for her."

Juan Carlos stood up and walked toward them. "As far as I'm concerned, you have earned this land. I want you to have it. You are truly one of us."

"Thank you. I'll take it." Nicholas smiled at the group. "Now if you don't mind, I think we need a few minutes alone."

He pulled her out onto the terrace connected with the dining room and there under the stars he drew her into his arms.

"Oh, Nicholas, you didn't have to prove anything to me," she murmured. "I know how difficult that must have been for you."

"I had to prove something to both of us. He reached into his pocket and pulled out his photograph. "And this is the final step." With one fluid motion he ripped the paper in two. "This picture isn't paradise, nor is that land out there. If this works out, that will be fine, but what I really need is you. Today when I walked on that beach, all I could think about was you and sitting around a table in the kitchen baking apple pie." He leaned over and kissed her lovingly on the lips, a promise of what was to come.

"Are you sure, Nick? We're so different."

"I know. Isn't it wonderful?"

"But I dance my way around the house."

"So I'll learn the side step."

"And you're going to hate the way I organize my shelves."

"I'll do it for you."

"My car will drive you crazy."

"I'll sell it and buy you a new one. None of that stuff matters anymore. I love you. But I've never had a family or anyone to love. I don't quite know how to..."

She put a finger to his lips. "I'll show you. Because I love you, too. Together we're going to make up for everything that we've missed in the past. And maybe someday we can build a house on a small portion of that beach out there and call it our paradise."

"Then you'll marry me?"

Her eyes brimmed over with happy tears as she smiled up at him. "Yes. But..."

"But what?" he asked warily.

"Only if you'll dance at our wedding."

"Are you kidding? I'll be there with bells on."

* * * * *

NORA ROBERTS

Love has a language all its own, and for centuries, flowers have symbolized love's finest expression. Discover the language of flowers—and love—in this romantic collection of 48 favorite books by bestselling author Nora Roberts.

Starting in February, two titles will be available each month at your favorite retail outlet.

In March, look for:

Irish Rose, **Volume #3**
Storm Warning, **Volume #4**

In April, look for:

First Impressions, **Volume #5**
Reflections, **Volume #6**

Collect all 48 titles and become fluent in

THE LANGUAGE of LOVE

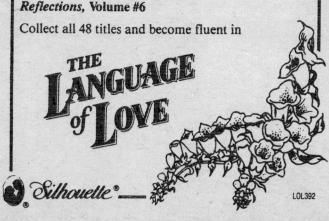

Silhouette®

LOL392

From the popular author of the bestselling title
DUNCAN'S BRIDE (Intimate Moments #349)
comes the

LINDA HOWARD

COLLECTION

Two exquisite collector's editions that contain four of
Linda Howard's early passionate love stories. To add
these special volumes to your own library, be sure
to look for:

VOLUME ONE: *Midnight Rainbow*
              Diamond Bay
              (Available in March)

VOLUME TWO: *Heartbreaker*
              White Lies
              (Available in April)

SLH92

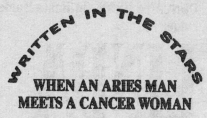

FOUL PLAY
AT DUSK

▶▶▶

She went to the open gate, and could see only moving lights; there was the noise of the train crews, distant voices. She had no idea how long the train would stay there; indeed, during the journey and many long stops thus far, there had been no way of knowing when the train would resume its jolting way. Off in the distance someone shouted hoarsely—and two strong hands shot out of the dusk below her, grasped her ankles and pulled.

She reached out toward the railing and clutched it as hard as she could, and then, instinctively and violently, tried to kick with the feet which were being dragged as if those two strong hands were determined to force her down.

Under the train, she thought coldly, for the train gave its usual premonitory jerk and puff that meant it was about to start again.

There was another jerk and the grip on her ankles tightened . . .

*   *   *